She nod

coming t

He tensed. *did?* "That's me, just the full-service landlord," he said, trying to keep the sarcasm out of his voice. He started to leave, but she put her hand on his arm.

"Jarrett, what I meant was you went beyond helping me." Her eyes searched his face. "I've asked far too much of you. BJ and I weren't part of the deal when you were ordered to move in here."

"Did you hear me complain?"

She shook her head. "You should. I feel like I've taken advantage."

"Like I said, I haven't minded."

"And I'm grateful for everything.…"

Grasping her hand on his arm, Jarrett leaned forward. The memory of last night's kiss had him aching for another. "I didn't do it for your gratitude, Mia."

Dear Reader,

So many of you have asked if I plan to give Jarrett McKane his own story. Well, I've finally returned to Winchester Ridge, Colorado, and decided the brooding, live-on-the-edge guy needs a little redemption.

It all starts when he runs into pregnant Mia Saunders and the tenants from Mountain View Apartments. There's widow Nola Madison, handyman and World War II vet Ralph Parkinson, and Joe Carson and other retirees like Emma and Charlie Lowery.

When Jarrett is court-ordered to move into his shambles of an apartment building, he finds himself going beyond landlord duties. He's talked into hanging Christmas lights, making runs to the hospital, painting a baby's nursery and standing in as a labor coach. Oh, yes, Jarrett McKane definitely meets his match.

In creating the characters of Nola, Emma, Ralph and Joe, it made me think back to my own grandparents, John and Lydgia Greiner, and Paul and Loretta Hannan. Their love was unconditional, and time with them was special. I hope this story brings back good memories for you, too.

Enjoy!

Patricia Thayer

PATRICIA THAYER
Daddy by Christmas

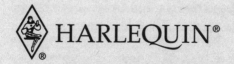
HARLEQUIN®

TORONTO • NEW YORK • LONDON
AMSTERDAM • PARIS • SYDNEY • HAMBURG
STOCKHOLM • ATHENS • TOKYO • MILAN • MADRID
PRAGUE • WARSAW • BUDAPEST • AUCKLAND

Recycling programs
for this product may
not exist in your area.

ISBN-13: 978-0-373-74067-3

DADDY BY CHRISTMAS

First North American Publication 2010

Originally born and raised in Muncie, Indiana, **Patricia Thayer** is the second of eight children. She attended Ball State University, and soon afterward headed west. Over the years she's made frequent visits back to the Midwest, trying to keep up with her growing family.

Patricia has called Orange County, California, home for many years. She enjoys not only the warm climate, but also the company and support of other published authors in the local writers' organization. For the past eighteen years she has had the unwavering support and encouragement of her critique group. It's a sisterhood like no other.

When she's not working on a story, you might find her traveling the United States and Europe, taking in the scenery and doing story research while thoroughly enjoying herself, accompanied by Steve, her husband for more than thirty-five years. Together they have three grown sons and four grandsons. As she calls them, her own true-life heroes. On her rare days off from writing, you might catch her at Disneyland, spoiling those grandkids rotten! She also volunteers for the Grandparent Autism Network.

Patricia has written for over twenty years and has authored more than thirty-six books for Silhouette and Harlequin Books. She has been nominated for both a National Readers' Choice Award and a prestigious RITA® Award. Her book *Nothing Short of a Miracle* won an *RT Book Reviews* Reviewer's Choice Award.

A longtime member of Romance Writers of America, she has served as president and has held many other board positions for her local chapter in Orange County. She's a firm believer in giving back.

Check her website at www.patriciathayer.com for upcoming books.

To my own little heroes, Harrison, Griffin, Connor and Finley. You're the light of my life.

CHAPTER ONE

SHE hated relying on a man.

Mia Saunders glanced around the filled-to-capacity community room at the Mountain View Apartments complex. It was already decorated for Thanksgiving and the tenants were hopeful that they would still be living here at the end of November.

At one of the many card tables were Emma and Charlie Lowery. They'd lived here for over twenty years. So had the Nordbergs, along with Second World War veteran and widower, Ralph Parkinson. They'd all come here for the same reason—affordable rent gave seniors on fixed incomes some independence.

At the age of twenty-nine, Mia was an exception, one of the few, younger tenants who lived in the aging apartment complex.

"You've got to help us, Mia!"

She turned to tiny, gray-haired Nola Madison standing beside her. She was a widow who had lived in the complex since her husband's death ten years ago. With social security and a small pension, Nola could survive living alone here without burdening her children.

"Nola, I'm going to try, but I'm not sure how much I can do."

"You're a lawyer," Nola said, her soft hazel eyes seeming larger behind her bifocals.

"Not yet. I've only just started law school." That had been put on hold this past semester and she had no idea when she could start up again.

"But you will talk to the owner for us when he gets here."

"*If* he gets here," Mia added. So far that hadn't happened. They'd tried a half-dozen times to have a meeting with the man to discuss the fifty-year-old apartment complex's crumbling condition. No improvements had been done in years.

"It seems the new owner has been avoiding us."

"Well, he has good reason. He doesn't want to fix things any more than the last owner." Joe Carson, another of the elderly tenants, spoke up behind her. That got the crowd going.

Mia waved her hand and they quieted down. "This isn't getting us anywhere. In all fairness..." She glanced down at the paper. "Mr.

Jarrett McKane only took possession of this property a few months ago."

"McKane," Nola repeated. "I wonder if he's any relation to the teacher at the high school, Kira McKane. My granddaughter, Hannah, talks about her all the time."

Joe stepped forward. "I don't care who he's related to, he has to take care of our demands."

Joe's wife, Sylvia, gasped. "What if he evicts us?"

That started more grumbles around the crowded room.

Mia eyed the tenants she'd gotten to know since coming to Winchester Ridge when her brother, Reverend Bradley Saunders, took over as pastor of the First Community Church a half mile away. She'd found a one-bedroom apartment in the affordable complex about three years ago when Brad and his wife, Karen, decided to make the small Colorado ranching community a permanent home. It was a perfect place for raising a family.

All Mia's life, it had been her brother who'd been there for her. Brad had never given up on his little sister, even when she gave up on herself. Over the years, he'd pulled her back from some pretty dark places, and let her know that she was important and loved. When their parents disowned her, Brad stood by her and helped her get her act together and get into college.

She'd do anything for him. Sadness washed over Mia, knowing she would never get the chance again.

Sam Parker hurried into the room and called out, "One of those fancy SUVs just pulled up. A shiny black one."

Those standing scurried to find a seat as if they'd been caught doing something wrong. Mia didn't rush much these days, but she felt the excitement and nervousness as she took a chair at the head table, and then turned her attention toward the door.

Nothing had prepared her for this man.

Jarrett McKane walked into the room as if he owned it. That was because he did. He was well over six feet, and his sheepskin jacket made him look ever bigger as his broad shoulders nearly filled the doorway. There was a brooding look in his ebony eyes that made him look intimidating.

It didn't work on her.

She was Preston Saunders's daughter. No one could intimidate like the CEO of a Fortune 500 company. Though there was no doubt that Jarrett McKane could give good old Preston a run for the title. Intimidator.

She released a breath and put on a smile. "Mr. McKane. It's good of you to come."

Jarrett turned toward her, his eyes showing some surprise and interest, and he returned a smile, showing off a row of straight white teeth. Oh boy. He was going to try to charm her.

"Ms. Saunders?"

"That would be me."

He walked to the table, pulling off his leather gloves then he held out his hand. "It's a pleasure to meet you, Ms. Saunders. I must say I've enjoyed your colorful letters."

She tried not to react as his large hand engulfed hers. *Get down to business,* she told herself and withdrew her hand.

"Well, they seem to have worked. You're here." She motioned to the chair across from her. "Please have a seat and we can begin."

Jarrett McKane didn't like this woman having the upper hand. Well, it wasn't going to last long. He eyed the pretty, long-haired brunette. Even tied back into a ponytail, those curls seemed to have a mind of their own. Her eyes caught his attention right off, a dark, smoky blue. She looked to be in her mid-twenties. He hated trying to guess women's ages, but he knew she was old enough.

He slipped off his jacket and she watched

with interest. He liked that. Maybe this would be easier than he thought.

Mia Saunders glanced down at the paper in front of her. "As I stated in my letters, Mr. McKane, there are several apartments that need your immediate attention. The bathrooms in several of the units aren't working properly, and many of the heaters aren't functioning at all. They're outdated and possibly dangerous." She looked up. "The conditions here are becoming unlivable, Mr. McKane." She slid the list across the table to him. "We need you to fix these items immediately."

Jarrett read over the itemized page. He already knew it would cost him a fortune. "And the previous owner should have taken care of these problems."

"Since you are the current owner, Mr. McKane, it's your responsibility now."

He glared at her.

She ignored it. "I'm sure you bought this property at a reduced price, and a good businessman would know the condition of the place. And since you are the owner now, we're asking that you please address these problems."

Jarrett glanced around at the group. He hadn't expected to find this when he arrived, especially not mainly senior citizens. He pushed away any sentimentality. "I can't fix these problems."

"Can't or won't?" she retorted.

"I don't see how that matters."

"It does to us, Mr. McKane."

"Okay, for one thing, I haven't received any rent payment since I took over the property."

"And you won't until we see some good faith from you. Some of these people don't have hot water or heat. Winter is here."

"Then relocating you all is the only answer." He stood. "Because in a few months, I'll be tearing the place down."

The group gasped, but Mia Saunders still looked calm and controlled as she said, "I don't think so, Mr. McKane."

Jarrett was surprised by her assertiveness. He wasn't used to that, especially not from a woman. No that wasn't true, his sister-in-law, Kira, gave him "what for" all the time.

Ms. Saunders held up another piece of paper. "We all have leases giving us six months to relocate. When you bought the building, your lawyer should have told you about it. Unless you didn't use an attorney."

Dammit, he didn't have an answer to that.

"And you still have to honor our leases."

He shook his head. "Can't do it. I want to start demolition by the first of the new year. And I'm sure the town council will go along with me since this is the site for a new computer-chip plant. It's estimated to bring over a hundred jobs to this town." He saw the panicked looks on the tenant's faces and added, "And I'll help anyone who wants to be relocated, but I can't let you stay here for six months." Finished, he headed toward the door.

"You might not have a choice," Mia called to him.

He turned around, perversely enjoying the exchange. He liked the fire in her pretty eyes, the set of her jaw. He wondered if he could find a way to sway her loyalty. A little dinner and maybe some romancing might help his cause. "I don't think you can win this fight, Ms. Saunders. But I'm willing to discuss it with you, another time."

She rose from her chair and that was when he noticed her rounded belly. Pregnant? Damn, she's pregnant.

Mia Saunders seemed to enjoy the surprise. "You can count on it, when we see you in court."

Thirty minutes later, Jarrett was still thinking about the attractive Mia Saunders as he drove his Range Rover down the highway. He shook his head. What the hell was he doing fantasizing about a pregnant woman? A woman carrying another man's baby.

He turned off onto the road leading toward the McKane ranch. After selling off his part of the family cattle ranch, he hadn't called in here much to start with. He and his half brother, Trace, hadn't gotten along while they were growing up, but the past few years that had slowly begun to change. Maybe he was getting soft. Of course, his brother's wife, Kira, had a lot to do with it.

Now, he was an uncle and he was crazy about his niece, Jenna. She could ask him to walk over hot coals, and he'd do it, smiling. At three years old, the toddler had his number.

He parked around the back of the house. They hadn't always been a happy family: he recalled just a while back when Trace and Kira were barely surviving a crumbling marriage. Kira's problems getting pregnant had put a strain on them that had nearly ended their five-year relationship. Then a miracle had happened, and now they had Jenna.

Climbing the back steps to the century-old ranch house, Jarrett's attention turned to another pregnant woman, Mia Saunders. It was true what they said about expectant mothers, they did have a glow about them. And unless he had been mistaken, she'd directed that rosy glow toward him.

He knocked on the door and walked in.

"Everyone decent?" He peered into the kitchen, knowing he'd be welcome. That hadn't always been true. There was a time he'd tried everything to one-up his younger brother. In their youth, he had wanted nothing to do with the ranch, or with the half brother who'd gotten all the attention. So, after their father died, Jarrett had accepted his share in dollars.

It had taken them years to work out their differences. And with the help of Kira and a sweet little girl named Jenna they'd worked through a lot of their problems, mainly just trying to be brothers.

Kira stood at the stove. "We have a three-year-old. There isn't any time to get indecent." His sister-in-law smiled as she came to him and gave him a kiss on the cheek. "Hi, Jarrett. It's good to see you."

"Hi, sis," he said, returning the hug. He'd used to have trouble with her being so demonstrative, but she said they were family, and that was how family acted.

Jarrett heard a squeal and little Jenna came charging into the room.

"Unca Jay. Unca Jay," the girl called.

Jarrett caught her up in his arms, swung her around, kissing her cheeks and blowing raspberries. "How's my Jenna girl today?"

The child's tiny mouth formed a pout. "Mommy put me in time-out. I was sad."

Kira arrived on the scene, brushing back her long blond hair. "Tell Uncle Jarrett what you did."

"I got into Mommy's makeup."

Suddenly, Jarrett could see the faint remnants of lipstick on her mouth. "Uh-oh."

"I just want to be pretty, like Mommy." She turned those big brown eyes on him. "Are you mad at me, too?"

"Never." He kissed her. "But you're already pretty, you don't need makeup." He glanced at Kira. "But remember you don't like anyone getting into your stuff, so you shouldn't get into other people's things."

"'Kay." She looked at her mom. "Can I play now? I promise to be good."

Kira nodded, and they watched the child run out of the room. She turned to Jarrett. "Thanks for backing me up."

He nodded. "I don't know how you ever punish her. It would tear me up."

"It part of being a parent."

"That's a job I don't want."

Kira smiled. "You just haven't found the right woman."

He arched an eyebrow. "I've found a lot of women and I like it that way. There's safety in numbers." He winked at her. "Among other things."

She shook her head. "Like I said, you haven't found the right woman."

"But I found mine."

They both looked toward the door to see Trace. His brother went straight to his wife and kissed her. Jarrett hated the envy that engulfed him. To his surprise, his thoughts turned to Mia Saunders again. Well, damn.

"Hi, bro," Jarrett greeted him. "How's the cattle business?"

"If you came out here more, you'd know for yourself."

"If I came out here more, you'd put me to work. You know how I feel about ranching. I'm doing just fine the way things are."

"I take it you're still trying to get by on your looks and your wit. So what brings you out here?"

Jarrett shrugged. "Do I need a reason?"

Trace hugged his wife close. "Of course not. Stay for supper."

Jarrett smiled. "Don't mind if I do." Whatever had happened during their childhood didn't seem to mean much anymore. It had taken years, but Jarrett had finally realized that Trace wasn't competing with him. After they'd found natural gas on McKane land a few years ago, they'd worked together and ensured a prosperous future for them all.

They also found they could be friends.

Kira went to check on Jenna while Trace poured two mugs of coffee. He handed one to Jarrett and the brothers sat down at the large farm kitchen table.

"So, I hear you bought the old apartment buildings on Maple."

Jarrett frowned. He'd been trying to keep the project quiet. "Where did you hear that?"

"It's a small town. There aren't many secrets."

Kira returned. "We heard it at church last Sunday. One of your tenants, her brother used to be our pastor. Reverend Brad Saunders." She shook her head. "It was such a tragedy about their deaths."

"I don't go to church. What happened to them?"

"A few months ago Brad and his wife, Karen, went on a missionary trip and their small plane crashed in Mexico. Poor Mia."

"What about her husband?

Kira raised an eyebrow. "Mia doesn't have a husband."

Interest sparked in Jarrett, catching him off

guard. "Surely the guy responsible for the baby will step up."

Kira exchanged a glance with Trace. "There is no guy to step up. It's not Mia's baby."

CHAPTER TWO

JARRETT stared at his sister-in-law. "Okay, it's been a few years since Biology 101, but I would remember something like this."

"Mia is a surrogate," she explained. "Or maybe I should say she was."

"There's definitely still a baby," he added, recalling the generous curve of her stomach.

"But no parents."

"So what's the story?"

Kira gave her husband a quick glance. "It wasn't exactly public knowledge, but Mia is carrying her brother and sister-in-law's baby."

"The hell you say!"

Suddenly Jenna came running into the kitchen. "Unca Jay, you said a bad word."

Jarrett ignored Trace's disapproving stare. "I'm sorry, sweetie," he told her. "I'll try to be better."

"You got to give me a nickel for the jar."

The child held out her tiny hand and smiled. "Pay me."

The little thief. With a smile he dug into his pocket. "Here's a quarter."

"Jenna, go wash up for supper," her mother said.

"Okay, Mommy." She smiled and went and hugged Trace. "Hi, Daddy."

While father and daughter exchanged pleasantries Jarrett tried to wrap his head around this news.

Once the child left, Jarrett turned back to Kira. "Was Mia Saunders going to give the reverend and his wife her baby?"

Kira shook her head. "No, she's been carrying Brad and Karen's baby all along. Surely you've heard of a fertilized embryo being implanted in another woman and she carries the baby when the biological mother can't. In this case, Mia was doing this for her brother and his wife."

Kira got up from the table, went to the oven and checked the roast, then she returned to the table. "But now everything has changed with Brad and Karen's death. Mia will not only be giving birth to her niece or nephew in about six weeks, but now she'll be raising the baby, too."

In the past, Jarrett had always run as far as possible from romantic entanglements. He didn't do relationships beyond a few months, no matter how beautiful or intriguing the woman. It would mean he'd have to put his feelings on the line, to be vulnerable—something he'd avoided since he'd been a kid when his mother had died. Still grieving, he'd soon learned that his father's new wife didn't want to deal with someone else's kid.

He'd concluded a long time ago he wasn't cut out to be a family man.

Yet, this woman caused him to pause. Why was he even giving her a second thought?

A woman with a baby?

He recalled the scene from earlier that day in the community room filled with all those elderly tenants and how Mia Saunders had led the pack. Those amazing blue eyes had dared him to challenge her demands. She'd tried to act tough, but he could see her nervousness.

"Does she have any other family?"

Kira shook her head. "From what I heard there was only her brother. Since her brother was a pastor, Brad and Karen didn't exactly have a fat bank account. Mia had been going to law school, but she had to drop out after the accident. I know she does Web design because she works from home, which is important now with the baby coming. The church is helping as much as possible."

And he was about to throw her out of her home. "When is the kid due?"

"Would you believe Christmas day?" Kira smiled. "I feel that's a good omen. I believe there's a miracle out there for her."

Jarrett hoped it happened before the New Year.

"They have the best food around," Jarrett told Neil Fulton the next afternoon at lunch. "Prime Cut's Barbecue is outstanding. It's all local beef, too. Some of it comes from my brother's ranch."

The fifty-five-year-old business executive looked as if he'd spent a lot of time behind a desk. His skin was pale and his hair thinning. "You own part of that, too?"

"No, I got out of ranching a long time ago." Jarrett hadn't liked all the hard work or a father who drove him to do more than a kid should have to do. For what? To wait out another drought, low cattle prices or a freezing winter without going bankrupt. And you're still poor. He liked the finer things in life, and he'd found a way to get them.

"But my brother is good at what he does. I guarantee you'll love the beef."

"Maybe another time, I usually eat a lighter lunch." Neil looked over his half-glasses at Jarrett. "My wife insists on it."

Jarrett would do everything he could to move this deal along. With the slow economy, he needed to make sure this sale didn't fall through. If only he could find a place for the Mountain View tenants, life would be perfect.

"Why not have the best of both worlds?" he said. "If you lived around here, you could enjoy hearty meals, because there's plenty of hiking and skiing around to keep you in shape. And there's a great gym where you can work out."

Neil smiled. "You've kept in shape well enough since you left football. How do you do it?"

Jarrett couldn't believe people still remembered his college career. But he'd use it if it helped seal the deal with Fulton Industries.

"I have a home gym," he explained. You and your wife will have to come by and I'll show you. It's Robin, isn't it?"

Fulton nodded, then returned to scanning the menu.

"I also want to show you both some houses in the area. There are several estates with horse property. Riding is another great way to keep in shape."

Neil raised a hand. "First, I need to put all my energy into building this plant. Robin will stay in Chicago until we can get things moving along. From past experience, once my wife gets going on a new house, she'll throw herself into decorating it."

"Well, when that happens I'll have one of my top agents help her find the perfect house."

Neil frowned. "You don't know Robin. She's hard to please."

Jarrett bet he could handle her. "Then I'll work with her personally."

Neil laughed. "You may live to regret that offer."

Before Jarrett could respond, a young man approached the table. "Excuse me, sir, are you Jarrett McKane?"

"Yes, I am."

The guy pulled out a manila envelope from inside his jacket. "This is for you." He smiled. "You've been served."

Jarrett felt his face heat with anger. Then he glanced across the restaurant as the man stopped at a table. He sat down beside a dark-haired woman. Mia Saunders.

"Is there a problem, Jarrett?" Neil asked.

"No. Just a minor disagreement with a client."

Mia raised a hand and waved.

"This doesn't have anything to do with our project, does it?"

Jarrett nodded at Mia. "Like I said it's a minor problem. Nothing I can't handle."

The following morning, Mia drove to her doctor's appointment in Grand Junction, about forty miles away. The roads were clear so far, and she only hoped that northwest Colorado's winter weather would hold off for another month.

Since she was in her last trimester, she had to travel there regularly. Not a problem; she liked her doctor, Lauren Drake. In her forties, the attractive fertility specialist had been there for her from the beginning of the surrogacy. She'd also supported Mia through Brad and Karen's horrible accident and death.

"How have you been feeling?"

"Great," Mia said. "Except the baby is pretty active. He or she is kicking all the time."

The attractive blonde was tall and slender and happily married to her college sweetheart. Mia should hate her for her perfect life, but Lauren was too nice to hate. She had become a good friend. And Mia needed as many friends as she could get.

"I know the pregnancy is going well, but I'm worried about you, Mia. Your life has been turned upside down in the past few months. And now, you aren't even sure about a place to live."

"So what else is new?" Sadness crept in. She missed her brother desperately. He'd been her rock for most of her life. Even with Brad's help, it had taken her years to get her act together. Now, she felt on the verge of falling apart. What kind of mother would that make her? Not a good one.

"I know you've had to deal with a lot," the doctor said. "You only planned to be the aunt to this baby. Now, you're going to be the mother, unless you've changed your mind on that."

Mia shook her head. Well before Brad and Karen had moved ahead with the surrogacy, everyone had agreed that if something ever happened to them, Mia would raise the child. Yet, no one had ever imagined the loss of both parents even before the baby arrived.

"It's a big responsibility, Mia. Even when there's a father in the picture."

Mia added, "A single mother with no money and no apparent means of income isn't the best candidate."

"Don't say that."

Mia hadn't hidden anything from the doctor before the procedure began. Dr. Drake knew about everything in her past.

"There are agencies around to help, too."

Mia shook her head. She had some money set

aside. And Brad and Karen had some left-over insurance money. "I just want a job."

"I'd prefer you didn't take any more on your plate right now."

Mia fought her panic. "Is there something wrong?"

Lauren shook her head. "Just watching your blood pressure. It's a little high, but no worries right now." She quickly changed the subject. "Have you picked out any names?"

"No, I haven't thought about it." She had some personal things of Karen's, a baby book that might give her a clue and a letter from her sister-in-law that Mia wasn't supposed to open until the birth of the baby.

"Well, do it. And stop trying to take on everyone's problems. Think about yourself for a change. You won't get the chance after the baby comes."

Mia knew she couldn't walk away from her neighbors. Not now. They'd been so good to her. "We're just trying to stay in our homes for a little while longer. We're going to court next week, and we're hoping the judge will rule in our favor."

Having a place to live was her main concern right now. She couldn't be homeless again. Not with a baby.

* * *

A week later, Jarrett walked into the courtroom. What he didn't expect to see were several of the tenants there, too. Of course, leading the pack was Mia Saunders.

She looked professional in her dark skirt and a long wine-colored sweater draped over her rounded stomach. Her rich brown hair was pulled back from her oval face and clipped at the base of her neck. She didn't wear makeup. She didn't try to highlight her already striking blue eyes or her rosy-hued lips. She did nothing to enhance her good looks. She didn't need to.

He wasn't interested in her anyway. She had issues he didn't want to deal with. Yet it seemed he would be dealing with her whether he liked it or not. He hoped today would end any and all future meetings.

That was why he'd brought his lawyer. Matthew Holliston wasn't only his attorney but a longtime friend from high school. And he was damn good at his job.

Although, when Matt had heard that Judge Barbara Gillard was going to hear the case, he'd been worried. She had a reputation as a tough judge, and something else went against Jarrett. Years ago, he had dated Judge Gillard's sister, Amy, in high school. It hadn't ended well, so Matt had suggested that he make a generous offer to the building tenants. They had written up something to appease the judge and, they hoped, the tenants.

"Good morning, Ms. Saunders," Jarrett said.

She nodded. "Mr. McKane."

He was quickly drawn into her sparkling gaze and lost the ability to say more. That was when Matt stepped in and guided him to his seat.

The court deputy soon called their case. "The Mountain View tenants versus Jarrett McKane Properties."

"Here, your honor," Matt acknowledged. He and Jarrett went to the front of the courtroom.

"We're also here, your honor." Mia Saunders walked up with two elderly people.

Everyone waited in silence as Judge Gillard glanced over the case papers in front of her. There were also pictures and estimates for several repairs. The judge's gaze turned to Jarrett. "How can you expect your tenants to live like this?"

Jarrett started to speak, but Matt stepped in. "Your honor, as you read in our deposition, my client only purchased the property three months ago."

The judge just looked at him, then said, "I assume, Mr. McKane, you did a walk-through of the property before purchasing it so you had to know the conditions. And if that wasn't enough,

Ms. Saunders contacted you several times. So you should have, at least, begun to make some of the repairs."

"Your honor," Matt tried again. "It would be a waste of time and money. Mr. McKane will be demolishing the building so a factory can be built there—a computer-chip plant that will bring several new jobs into the area."

"Your honor," Mia Saunders interrupted. "The tenants had to sign a lease agreement when they moved in. It states that if the property is ever sold they have six months to relocate." She flashed a cold stare at Jarrett, then went on. "Even with the change of ownership, until each tenant is contacted about their eviction, they still have five months and three weeks to stay in their apartments."

Matt fought back. "Your honor, isn't six months a little excessive? A thirty-day notice is a standard agreement now."

The judge looked at the lease in her hand. "Well, this agreement *is* from 1968." She glanced over her glasses. "But no one thought to change it." She held up the photos. "I'm more concerned that many of these apartments aren't suitable to live in."

Nola stepped forward and introduced herself. "Your honor, I'm Nola Madison, one of the long-time tenants. May I speak?"

The judge nodded. "Yes, Mrs. Madison, you may."

The tiny woman made her way to the front. "Many of us have lived at Mountain View Apartments for a long time. It's our home, and like all of us, it's getting old. With a little work and some minor repairs, we can live comfortably for the winter. Please don't ask us to leave yet."

"You know that in six months you will have to move anyway," the judge told her.

Nola glanced around to her group of friends and neighbors. "Next week is Thanksgiving, your honor. For years a lot of us have spent it together. Christmas, too. If this is our last year, I really would like to be with my friends. My family. And we need the time to find affordable places to live and to save the extra money to move. So staying until March would be helpful."

Seeing the judge blink several times, Jarrett knew he was in big trouble.

"Your honor," Matt tried again. "This is not a good situation, but there is an important business deal pending here. A factory is to be built on this site. A factory that will bring jobs into our community."

The judge straightened. "From which your client will benefit nicely, I'm sure. While these people will lose their homes." She glared daggers toward Jarrett. "Mr. McKane, you knew the conditions of the lease, and you also knew the deplorable condition of the building when you made the purchase."

He didn't agree or disagree. "What I had planned was to help the tenants relocate," he replied.

The judge wasn't buying it. "Seems to me if you'd been sincere you would have answered their letters three months ago," she observed. "Now you're throwing them out of their homes as though nothing matters as long as you make a profit. Well, it's not always about profit, Mr. McKane. My ruling is that you make the necessary repairs to bring the building up to code. I'll waive the fine as long as you begin immediately."

Jarrett bit the inside of his mouth. "Yes, your honor."

"Don't think that's all there is, Mr. McKane. You're to make all repairs so the place is livable." Judge Gillard paused and looked at Mia Saunders. "Is there a vacant apartment?"

Mia nodded. "Yes, your honor, but the apartment is unlivable."

The judge nodded. "Good. What's the number?"

"Two-oh-three-B."

"Jarrett McKane, I order you to move into apartment 203B at Mountain View complex until all repairs are completed. No eviction until March first. Although, I do want to see you back here after the holidays to learn about your progress." She hit the gavel on the block. The sound echoed around the courtroom. "Court adjourned."

"Judge, this is highly irregular," Matt called, but she had already exited the courtroom.

That left Jarrett thinking about everything he was about to lose. No, he couldn't lose this. He'd fix this, like he'd fixed everything all his life. He'd figure out a way to get what he wanted. He always did.

The next day, Jarrett and Matt parked in front of the Mountain View Apartments. "You can't bend any of the rules, Jarrett," Matt told him. "You have to sleep here every night, eat here and even work here. You can only go to your home to get more clothes and food, that's all, or the judge could toss you in jail. You know she means business when she instructed me to escort you here personally."

"Dammit, Matt, you'd better get me out of this mess. If Fulton finds out, he'll walk away from the deal."

"Well, unless he'll wait until April, you're

in big trouble. The only alternative you have is talking them into moving out."

Jarrett was frustrated. Thanks to Mia Saunders, he had to figure out something. But honestly there weren't many options since housing was limited in Winchester Ridge.

He looked toward the yellow-and-brown structure with the peeling paint and sagging rain gutters. It seemed even worse with winter-bare trees, but the grass was cut and the hedges trimmed.

"In its day, the place was probably a show-case," Matt observed.

"Well, it's not 1960," he told his friend. "And I'm only going to do the minimum that needs to be done. It's a waste of time and money."

Jarrett looked out the Mercedes' windshield to see someone coming toward them. It was the older woman, Mrs. Madison. He pressed the button so the window went down.

"Hello, Mr. McKane." She slowly made her way to the car. "I'm not sure if you remember me, I'm Nola Madison."

He got out of the car. "Were you checking up to see if I was coming?"

She smiled despite his rudeness. "As a matter of fact, we were watching for you, but only to warn you about what to expect in your apartment." She shook her head. "It was once the manager's, but he didn't take very good care of it. We tried the best we could to clean it up." She held out a key dangling from a heart keychain. "But I'm afraid it needs more work than any of our places."

Feeling like a heel, Jarrett took the key from her, and pulled his jacket together against the cold. "You shouldn't be out in this weather, Mrs. Madison."

"Please, call me Nola. Let's go inside, but it isn't much warmer."

Jarrett grabbed his duffel bag from the back of the car, asked Matt to have his car brought over from the office, and followed the woman up the walk. They went into a bare lobby. He'd seen this area before and knew how bad it looked, but it hadn't mattered to him, since it was tagged for demolition. He headed for the elevators to find signs that read, Out of Order.

On the walk-through of the property he hadn't noticed that. "There is no elevator?"

She shook her head. "Not in the last year."

Jarrett recalled that day in the community room—two of the tenants were in wheelchairs. "How do the handicapped get upstairs?"

She led him to the wrought-iron staircase and they started the climb. "Oh, we found two tenants who were willing to move upstairs, and Joe and Sylvia's son, Ryan, built ramps for both

Margie and Harold. Now they can get in and out or their apartments. It's important to be independent."

"Who exchanged apartments?"

"Well, Mia was one who moved upstairs, and when her brother, Reverend Brad, was alive he used to help us with a lot of repairs. Many of his congregation did, too."

"Where was the owner? Some of these repairs are required by law."

She shook her head. "He threatened to double our rent if we kept complaining. So we started fixing things ourselves." They made it to the second floor. "But some things we can't fix. We need an expert."

Once again he was confronted with dingy walls and worn carpet. They passed a few doors, then she stopped in front of his apartment. He paused. Hell, he was afraid to go inside.

Suddenly the door across the hall opened and Mia Saunders stepped out. She actually smiled at him and he felt a strange tightness in his chest. "Moving in, Mr. McKane?"

She was dressed in a long blue sweater that went to midthigh, with a pair of black leggings covering those long legs. He looked back at her face. "Seems I am. Looks like we're going to be neighbors."

"Isn't that nice," Nola said, then glanced at

her watch. "Oh, my, I just remembered I have a doctor's appointment. I don't know where my head is today. Mia, could you show Mr. McKane around?"

Mia frowned. "Do you need a ride, Nola?"

"No, thank you, dear, my daughter is coming by." With a wave, the older woman walked off.

Mia didn't like Nola's not-so-subtle disappearing act. Why did anyone need to show Jarrett McKane around?

She walked to the apartment entrance. "Brace yourself." She swung open the door, reached in and flicked on the lights, then motioned for him to go inside first. He frowned and stepped into the main room. She heard his curse and couldn't help but smile as she followed him in.

The apartment walls needed paint, but not before numerous holes in the plaster were patched. Under the slipcovers that Nola and her welcoming committee had recently put on, the furniture was thrift-store rejects.

"Joe cleaned the carpet, or what's left of it. It's probably the original. At least the place doesn't smell as if someone died in here anymore."

Without comment, he continued down the hall and peered into the bath. Again another curse.

She called after him. "It might not look very good, but I can guarantee you Nola and Sylvia cleaned it within an inch of its life. And there are fresh towels. And they made up the bed for you, too." Then she murmured to herself, "Why they're being so nice to you, I have no idea."

The good-looking Jarrett McKane came out and stood in front of her. His dark hair had been cut and styled recently. His clothes were top-of-the-line, too. Everything about him rang out success and power. So why was she even noticing him?

Hormones, she concluded. It was just late-pregnancy hormones. She'd learned a long time ago to stay away from men like him.

"Why did they do all this?" he finally asked.

Jarrett McKane was standing too close, but she refused to step back. She refused to let him intimidate her.

"It's their way of being neighborly," she told him. "It's the same with everyone here. Over the years, they've all become a family. Some are alone. Some have family that didn't have time for them so they take care of each other."

"Or it's their way to get me to not tear the place down."

She smiled, not wanting him to see her anger. "It's just some towels and linens and a few home-cooked meals. But yes, they feel it's worth a try.

Enjoy your stay." She turned and started to leave when he called her name.

When she turned around, he gave her a sexy grin. "Did you do anything to sway me, Ms. Saunders?"

Her heart began to pound in her chest. "There might be a plate of oatmeal raisin cookies on the kitchen counter."

"I'm looking forward to seeing how far you'll go to persuade me."

Mia arched her aching back, causing her stomach to be front and center. "I'm afraid cookies are as far as I'm willing to go."

CHAPTER THREE

MIA couldn't get out of there fast enough.

She stepped inside her apartment and closed the door. She didn't want Jarrett McKane in her life, or in her space. And he was suddenly in both.

A long time ago, she'd learned about men who thrived on control. Her father was one of those. It had taken her years to get out from under his reign and finally to be free of him.

She walked across her cozy living area. A secondhand sofa and chair faced the small television. A triangular rug hid a lot of the worn carpet underneath. A small table off the galley kitchen was used for eating and for working on her computer.

Her laptop was the only thing of value that she had and the only means she had these days of make a living. Despite her privileged upbringing, she'd never been materialistic. Maybe that was the reason it had been so easy to walk away, or in her case, run away.

To Preston and Abigail Saunders their daughter had always been a problem, a disappointment from the start. An overweight child, Mia had morphed into a rebellious teenager. She had never fitted into her Boston society family. So, once she was of age, she'd just disappeared from their lives.

Even Brad had eventually bucked their father's plans for him. Instead, her older brother had became an ordained minister and had ended up disowned, too.

Now she'd lost her only family. She caressed her stomach, feeling the gentle movement of the baby. At least she'd have a part of Brad and Karen and she vowed to love and protect this child. So she wasn't about to let her parents know where she was. Or let them find this baby.

Mia sat down in the chair, still in awe of the life she carried inside her. Onetime wild child, Margaret Iris Ashley Saunders was going to have a baby. She blew out a breath. She was going to be a mother and D-day was approaching soon. There were so many things she had to get done before Christmas.

She closed her eyes. For months, she'd had to push aside all the feelings she was having for this baby. A mother's feelings. The only thing that had saved her was knowing this child would always be in her life. Brad and Karen would have been the perfect parents and she could be the favorite aunt who spoiled the child.

Now, Mia had to step up and be a parent to this baby. She wasn't sure she was cut out to do it.

That afternoon, with the help of his office staff, Jarrett had made several phone calls. He'd finally found someone to start on the repairs. A local furnace repairman was to come out. He'd also contacted the handyman who serviced some of his other properties to help out with some of the minor fixes.

Flipping his phone shut, he decided to wait downstairs and get out of his depressing apartment for a while. In the hall, the door across from his opened and Mia walked out carrying a large trash bag. She stiffened the second she saw him.

He smiled. "Hello, Mia."

She nodded stiffly. "Mr. McKane."

She was dressed in her standard black pants and over-size blouse, but with an added long sweater for warmth.

"I don't see why we can't be on a first-name basis since we're going to be neighbors."

"You're the man who's evicting us. Why would I get friendly with the enemy?"

He took the bag from her. "It doesn't seem to bother the others." He gave her a sideways glance. "Someone must have really have done a number on you."

She glanced away. "Now you're a psychiatrist?"

"No, just observant."

"Well, observe somewhere else. Thanks to you, I have a lot on my mind."

He wasn't crazy about having to move her in her condition. "I'm not your enemy, Mia. I'm trying to find all of you places to live."

"We can't afford most of the other places."

Was that his fault? "The rent here is well below average for this area. Even if I kept the place and did all the repairs, I'd have to raise the rent."

"Well, you can't yet. Some of us are barely getting any heat or hot water."

"I'm taking care of that."

"I can't tell you how many times we heard that from the last owner."

"The last owner hadn't been court-ordered," Jarrett said. He slowed his pace so she could keep up. He knew little or nothing about pregnant women. Only that Kira had had a rough time with her pregnancy and had had to stay in bed the last few months.

"That's where I'm going now," he continued, "to meet with a furnace guy."

She stopped. "You mean we could have some heat today?"

He shrugged. "I'm paying him extra to start right away."

They continued their way down the stairs to the main lobby. "I would like to ask a favor," he said.

She paused with a glare.

He hid a smile as he raised a hand. "Good Lord, woman, do you mistrust everyone? I only want you to help get everyone together so we see who has the worst problems and fix them first."

"Then come to the community room. It's where a lot of the tenants hang out because it has a working heater."

They stepped outside into the frigid weather. He first tossed the sack into the Dumpster, and then they continued on to the center.

"I hear your baby is due on Christmas day."

She gave him a sideways glance. "Who told you that?"

"My sister-in-law, Kira McKane. You both go to the same church."

She seemed relieved. "How does she feel about you tossing us out of here?"

"I haven't tossed out anyone, and according to the judge, I won't be able to until the spring." Not with Barbara Gillard watching him anyway. If only he could come up with a way to convince everyone to leave a few months earlier.

His only other chance was to get Fulton to hold off on the takeover date. They couldn't begin construction until the ground thawed. But he wouldn't get his money either.

He'd put a lot into this project, buying up the surrounding land, including this place. He had too much to lose. And it would cost him even more every day Mountain View Apartments stayed open. And now he was being held prisoner here.

While Jarrett went to the community room, Mia knocked on Joe's door and asked him and Sylvia to gather the other tenants and bring them to the community room.

Sending the others on ahead, Mia then went to Nola's place and they walked over together. "We need to make sure you have enough heat, Mia," Nola said. "For you and the baby."

They went through the door of the community room to see a dozen or so tenants already there. "I'm fine for now," Mia answered. Her apartment wasn't too bad. "I wouldn't mind a new faucet for the sink, though. It came off last week."

"You should have told Joe."

"I wasn't going to complain when there are apartments with bigger problems."

Nola gave her a tender look. "You and the baby are a priority."

Mia smiled. Everyone here had rallied around her like overprotective grandparents since they'd heard the tragic news. "He's not even here yet."

"It's a boy?" Joe said, walking over to them.

"I don't know," she insisted. "So you haven't won the baby pool yet."

The older man grinned. "It's a boy all right. He's going to be born at 12:05 on the twenty-fifth of December."

Mia looked up to see Jarrett walk in, followed by a middle-aged man with Nichols Heating and Air printed across his shirt pocket.

"Good, most of you are here," Jarrett began. "This is Harry Nichols. He's here to look at the heating units."

Several of the tenants were already on their feet to greet the repairman. Once the niceties were over, the tenants commandeered Harry and went to start the work.

With everyone gone, Jarrett walked over to

where Mia sat at the table. "That seemed to please them."

She studied her new landlord. He was sure proud of himself. "Why not? It's been a while since they've had reliable heat. You'll probably be rewarded with some more baked goods."

Jarrett took a seat next to her, filling the space with his large frame. She inhaled a faint scent of his aftershave.

"I had no idea the extent of the last owner's neglect. I thought it was mostly cosmetic. Now, I'm paying a lot for the repairs."

Mia eyed his expensive clothes, leather jacket and cowboy boots. She'd seen his top-of-the-line Range Rover parked out front. "I doubt you'll starve, Mr. McKane. Besides, this isn't your only property in town."

He arched an eyebrow. "The last I heard, it's not against the law to make a living."

"No. Not unless the properties have been neglected like this one."

He looked at her with those dark, piercing eyes. "In the first place, I wasn't the one who allowed this property to fall apart. Secondly, most of my other holdings are commercial buildings. I've spent a lot of money renovating run-down properties. You can't ask for top rent without a quality product."

Why couldn't he do the same here? "Have

you ever considered putting money into this place? You have a whole other section that's vacant. That's twenty-four units that are empty." She shrugged. "Like you said yourself, this town doesn't have enough rental properties. With some remodeling you could sell them as townhomes."

He studied her for a while. "Sounds like you've put some thought into this."

"When we heard that the owner was selling, the tenants tried to buy the complex themselves. They didn't have enough money, or the expertise to do the repairs."

"I doubt if anyone can keep up with the repairs of this old place. No one would want to sink the time and effort into it, without knowing if they could recoup their money. The real estate market has been unpredictable."

He sounded like her father. "Does it always have to be about money?"

He arched an eyebrow. "It does or I go broke."

She'd been both, and she was definitely happier like this. "I can't believe you'd lose everything. You still have family and a home. You might lose a little money, but you'll survive. A lot of these people won't. They can't afford to move and pay double the rent elsewhere."

He frowned. "What are you going to do when the lease is up?"

She blinked, fighting her anger. "Is your conscience suddenly bothering you about evicting a single mother?"

He straightened. "I'm not happy about evicting anyone. But I don't have a choice. This deal has been in the works for months."

"Like I said, it's all about the almighty dollar."

"What about the jobs this factory will create for the town? The economy isn't that great to turn this opportunity away."

"Does a factory have to be built on land that drives people from their homes?"

"I will find them other places to live. I'm not that cruel—I won't put seniors and single mothers out on the street."

"Well, you can stop worrying about me. I don't want your charity."

"Fine. Let's see where your stubbornness gets you."

"I've been able to take care of myself so far."

"Then feel free to continue." He stood and started to leave.

She tried not to let him see her fear. She raised her chin. "I will."

Suddenly she felt her stomach tighten and she automatically covered it with her hands.

He must have seen it, too. "Are you okay?"

She nodded as she moved her hand over her belly and rubbed it, but it didn't help. Then her back began to hurt, too. She tried to shift in the chair, but it didn't help.

"Mia, what's wrong?" Jarrett asked.

She shook her head. "Nothing."

He knelt down beside her chair. "The hell it's nothing."

She shook her head, looking around the empty room. There wasn't anyone else there.

His expression softened. "Mia, let me help you."

A sharp pain grabbed her around the middle. "Oh, no," she gasped and then looked at him. "I think the baby's coming."

Fifteen minutes later Jarrett pulled up at the emergency-room doors. He threw the car into Park, got out and ran around to the passenger side. He jerked open the door. Mia was taking slow measured breaths. Not good.

"Hang on, we're almost there."

She couldn't hide her worried look. "It's too early for me to go into labor. I can't lose this baby, Jarrett."

"And you won't," he promised. He had no idea

what was going on, or even if the doctors could stop the contractions. "Let's get you inside and find some help." He slid his arms around her shoulders and under her legs, then lifted her into his arms.

"I'm too heavy," she said.

"Are you kidding?" He smiled, taking long strides across the parking lot. "During roundup, I used to have to hoist calves a lot heavier than you."

"You used to work on your brother's ranch?"

"Back when I played cowboy, it was our dad's place. That was a long time ago."

She studied him. "I can see you as a rancher."

His mouth twitched. "There's the big difference, darlin'. I never did," he drawled as he carried her through the automatic doors.

On the drive over, Mia had phoned her doctor and been told to go to the nearest emergency room, then she'd given Nola a quick call so her friends wouldn't worry if they noticed she was gone.

Winchester Ridge Medical Center was the closest. Once inside, they were met by a nurse who led them into an exam room. Jarrett set Mia down on the bed and stepped back out of the way. Nurses immediately took her blood pressure, asking questions about due dates and the timing of the contractions. All the while, she kept looking at him.

Jarrett tried to give her some reassurance, but he didn't know what to say.

"Excuse me," a nurse said, getting his attention. "Are you the father?"

He shook his head, but hesitated with the answer. "No." Mia didn't have any family.

"Then you'll have to leave while we examine her."

"I'll be right outside," he told Mia. "Just holler if you need me."

Jarrett stepped back behind the curtain and found a row of chairs against the wall. That was as far as he was going.

For the next few hours, Jarrett watched medical personal go in and out of Mia's cubicle.

But no one told him a thing.

Finally they moved her down the hall to a room so they could keep monitoring her. Recalling the frightened look on her face, he knew he couldn't leave her alone. So he followed her and camped outside her room.

He glanced up from the newspaper someone else had left and saw Nola.

He stood as the older woman walked toward

him. "Mr. McKane." She gripped his hand with both of hers. "How is Mia?"

"I don't know any more than what I told you when I phoned. And the doctor won't tell me anything because I'm not a relative."

Nola nodded. "I know, I fibbed and said I was her grandmother so I could come back here."

He walked Nola to the sofa and sat down. "How did you get here?"

"One of the parishioners from the church," she said. "Joe can't drive at night, and Ralph doesn't have his license any more." She shook her head. "Mia always takes us places we need to go." The older woman blinked. "Oh, Mr. McKane, what if something is wrong with the baby?" Those watery hazel eyes turned to him. "She wants this baby so much."

He already knew that. He'd never felt so helpless and he hated that. "Nola, the doctors here are good and her specialist is here, too. So try not to worry." He put on a smile. "And will you do me another favor? Please call me Jarrett."

She beamed at him.

He'd broken one of his cardinal rules. Not to get personally involved when it came to business. A week ago if someone told him he'd be sitting here worried about a pregnant woman and a couple of dozen retirees, he'd have told them they were crazy.

An attractive blond woman in a white coat came down the hall toward them. "Are you waiting to hear about Mia Saunders?"

They both stood. "Yes, we are," Jarrett said. "I'm Jarrett McKane, I brought Mia in. This is Nola Madison, her...grandmother. How is she?"

The doctor smiled. "Nice to meet you both. I'm Lauren Drake, Mia's doctor. She's fine for now. We managed to stop the contractions, but I want her to stay overnight as a precaution."

"What about the baby?" Nola asked.

"The fetus is thirty-four weeks, so if Mia does go into labor, she could deliver a healthy baby. Of course the longer she carries it, the better."

"Well, we'll do everything we can to make sure of that," Nola said.

The doctor nodded. "I'm glad, because when she goes home, I want her to stay in bed for the next few weeks. She needs to avoid all stress and just rest."

No stress, Jarrett thought. *Great.* He'd dumped a truckload on her. "Is that what caused the contractions?"

"We all have to agree that a lot has happened to Mia in the past few months," the doctor echoed. "Losing her brother and sister-in-law was traumatic for her."

Nola spoke up. "We've all been trying to help her through it."

Dr. Drake nodded. "I hope that can continue, because she's going to need someone to be around more, or at least within shouting distance to check on her."

"We can be there as much as she needs us," Nola said and turned to him. "Right, Jarrett?"

Great, he was the last person Mia wanted around. "Of course. I live across the hall. I guess I could keep an eye on her."

Thanks to the medication, Mia was feeling groggy. She didn't like that. For years, she'd avoided any and all drugs. But if it kept the baby safe, she'd do whatever it took.

Closing her eyes, she wondered how she was going to manage over the next few weeks. She had deadlines to make, and she needed the money.

Stop! Worrying wasn't good for the baby. She rubbed her stomach, knowing how close she'd come to delivering early. She wasn't ready for the baby. She didn't even have any diapers and very few clothes. The baby bed wasn't set up, either. She sighed. How was she going to do everything? How could she do everything and be a good mother, too? A tear slid down her cheek.

She thought back to her childhood. She'd always messed up. How many times had her father told her that? She couldn't please him no matter how hard she tried. He'd been too busy for her, but the one way she got his attention was being bad. Until he finally gave up on her altogether. No she couldn't let Brad down. She was going to be a good mother to his baby.

Mia glanced toward the door and saw Nola and Jarrett standing there. She quickly wiped away any more tears and put on a smile.

"Hi."

Nola rushed in. "Oh, sweetheart," she cried. "How are you?" Nola hugged her.

Mia relished the feeling, the love and compassion. "I'm doing better now."

The older woman pulled back. "We were so worried about you."

Mia looked at Jarrett. "I didn't want you to worry."

Nola frowned. "Of course we'd worry. You are special to us. We love you." She fussed with the blanket, smoothing out the wrinkles. "And we're going to take good care of you. Aren't we, Jarrett?"

"Looks that way," he said, feeling awkward standing in the room.

"I can't impose on either of you."

"You're not imposing on any of us. We're

happy to do it. You need someone around to help you. Jarrett and I volunteered." She clutched her hands together. "Oh, I need to go and call the others. I'll be right back."

"Here, use my phone," Jarrett said, handing it over to her. They both watched the woman walk out of the room.

Jarrett turned back to Mia. "So how do you really feel?"

"Scared, but good."

"You need to stop that. Your doctor said you need to relax and avoid stress."

"Did you tell her that you lived across the hall?"

He fought a smile, but lost. "Yes. Did you tell her that you and your friends brought me there?"

She met Jarrett's gaze. Her heart sped up and the monitor showed it. "So, I guess we're stuck with each other for a while."

CHAPTER FOUR

THE next day, Mia arrived home the same way she'd left. In Jarrett's car. He pulled into a parking spot at the front of the building. There were two heating-and-air-conditioning-repair trucks there, along with several uniformed workers.

"Looks like we'll have heat soon," she said.

Jarrett turned off the engine and glanced out the windshield. "It's just in time. There's a snowstorm coming in tonight." He looked at her. "Soon you'll be tucked into your warm bed. But be warned, Nola is heading a welcome-home committee."

"Oh, I don't want them to go to any trouble."

"I doubt they think you're any trouble. Too bad she and her group don't run this town. A lot more would get done." He climbed out of the SUV and walked around to her side.

He pulled open the door and the cold air hit

her. She shivered as she tried to climb out, but he wouldn't let her.

"Remember what the doctor said? Bed rest."

"I will as soon as I get to my apartment."

"No, as soon as I get you to your apartment." He scooped her up into his arms.

"Please, you can't carry me all the way upstairs."

"Of course not. Once I get you inside, Joe's going to take over."

She made a face at him. "Very funny."

Mia refused to admit she liked being taken care of by a big, strong man whose mere presence made her aware she was a woman. The way he smelled, his rock-solid chest and arms. She bit back a groan. Hormones. It was all just hormones.

She had to think of Jarrett McKane as the man who would be kicking them all out of their homes in a few months. Nothing more.

Sylvia held open the door to the building so they could come in. "Welcome home, Mia."

She got more greetings from a group of tenants waiting in the lobby.

"Thank you everyone. It's good to be home."

"Okay, let's get you upstairs." Jarrett continued to the stairway to her apartment.

Nola was waiting there and motioned him toward the bedroom. "Bring her in here."

"No, I can stay out here on the sofa for now."

Jarrett stopped, then said, "Doctor's orders are to put you to bed." He continued through the short hallway and into her room.

Mia blinked as they entered the bedroom. It didn't look like the same room she'd left yesterday. The dingy walls had been painted a soft buttery yellow. The furniture was rearranged and her bed was adorned with a pastel-patterned quilt.

She turned around and saw the white baby bed that had been Brad and Karen's last purchase for the baby assembled. It was decorated with yellow-and-green sheets and an animal mobile hung overhead.

Tears flooded her eyes. "Oh, my."

"Do you like it?" Nola asked. We were going to give you the quilt for Christmas but since you're going to be spending so much time in bed now, we decided not to wait." The older woman pulled back the covers so Jarrett could set her down on the snowy-white sheets.

"Oh, it's beautiful." She examined the intricate work. "How could you get all this done? I've only been gone overnight."

Nola exchanged a look with Jarrett. "We knew

we had to. The scare yesterday made us realize that you've been working so hard for us, you put off getting ready for the baby." She helped Mia take off her shoes and put her feet under the blanket. "So we hope this helps you to stop worrying so much." She stood back. "And when you've rested I'll show you all the baby clothes we've collected."

Nola walked to a small white dresser. "Joe found this for you. He sanded and painted it last week and Jarrett helped bring it up. Sylvia and I washed all the baby things and put them inside. If you don't like how we arranged them, you can change it."

"I'm sure it will be perfect." Mia clasped her hands together. "I don't know what to say."

"You don't have to say anything." The older woman came to the bed and hugged her. "Just take care of yourself. We love you, Mia. You're like family."

"I love you all, too."

She'd tried for a lot of years not to get too close to people, except for Brad. Starting with her parents. Whenever she'd let people in, they'd ended up hurting her. She looked across the room at Jarrett standing in the doorway. She definitely had to keep this man away.

"Tell everyone thank you."

"I will," Nola assured her. "Now, you rest and

don't worry about lunch. Sylvia will be here to fix you something."

"She doesn't have to do that."

Nola raised her hand. "She wants to. We all want to help." The older woman went out the door, followed by Jarrett. Mia called him back. "Mr. McKane, could I speak to you a moment?"

Frowning, he came toward the bed as Nola left. "Suddenly I'm Mr. McKane again."

"I appreciate everything you've done for me. It's better if we don't become too friendly... given the situation."

He studied her for a moment. "The situation you are referring to is that you've already gotten to stay here until the spring." He shrugged. "But, hey, I won't bother you again."

He turned and walked out. The soft click of the front door let her know she was truly alone. She told herself it was better this way. She couldn't get any more involved with a man like Jarrett McKane. Not that she had to worry that he'd ever give her a second look.

She rubbed her stomach. All she needed to focus on right now was her baby.

Jarrett kept hearing a ringing sound. He blinked his eyes as he reached for his cell phone on the bedside table.

"Hello," he murmured, running a hand over his face. It was still dark outside.

"Oh, I'm sorry, did I wake you?"

It was Mia. He sat up. "Mia? Is there a problem?"

"No. No. I shouldn't have bothered you."

"Wait, Mia. Tell me what's wrong. Is it the baby?"

"No, the baby's fine. I just need a favor, but I'll call back later."

"I'll be right over." He hung up, grabbed a pair of jeans and put them on along with a sweatshirt. He grabbed his keys and phone and headed across the hall. He let himself into her apartment with his master key and hurried to the bedroom.

Mia was sitting on the bed, dressed in a thermal long-sleeved shirt that hugged her rounded belly and a pair of flannel pajama bottoms. Somehow she managed to look somewhere between wholesome and far too good at this time in the morning.

Was it morning? "What's the problem?"

She looked embarrassed. "I'm so sorry I woke you."

"Well, since you have, tell me what you need."

"Could you pull out the table and see if my

cable is plugged in? I didn't want to move the table by myself."

"You're on the computer at this hour?"

She shrugged. "I slept so much during the day, I'm wide-awake. So I thought I'd get some work done."

Jarrett went to the bedside table and pulled it out. Seeing the loose battery cable, he knelt down and pushed it back into the outlet. "It's fixed." He moved the table back and stood next to the bed. "You're really not supposed to be working."

"I'm bored. Besides, if I don't work, I don't eat or pay my rent."

The computer screen lit up and he asked, "What are you working on?"

She kept her focus on the screen. "A Web site for a Denver-based company."

He glanced at the home-page logo. "Are you going back to law school?"

As she clicked the mouse and another program opened, she didn't show any surprise that he knew her history. "Not for a while, but I hope I can go back someday. It won't be easy with a baby."

"I'm sure everyone here would love to help you."

"We won't be living here...together," she said.

When she looked up at him with her scrubbed-clean face, large sapphire eyes and her hair in a ponytail, she looked fifteen. "How old are you?"

Mia blinked at his question. "Don't you know you're not supposed to ask a woman her age?"

He shrugged. "You look like jailbait."

"I'm twenty-nine. How old are you?"

"Thirty-seven."

She studied him for a few seconds. "You look it."

Frowning, he combed his fingers through his hair. "What's that supposed to mean?"

"What did you mean when you called me jailbait?"

"I meant it as a compliment. You look young for your age."

"Thank you." She sobered. "Are you really going to try and find us all a place to live?"

"I'm not sure I can find everyone a place, but I'll see what I can do." Was he crazy? Where would he find affordable apartments for them all? He moved away from the bed. "Man, I'd kill for a cup of coffee."

"Sorry, I'm off caffeine for a while," she told him. "But I'd fight you for a jelly donut."

"I guess that's one of those crazy cravings, huh? Well, I'd better go." He walked out, thinking a donut didn't sound so bad.

He retrieved his car keys and a jacket from his apartment and headed down to his car. The ground was covered in a dusting of snow. He climbed into his vehicle, missing the warm garage back at his house. Pushing aside his discomfort, he started the engine and the heater. He was on a quest for one hungry pregnant woman.

In every town there always seemed to be a twenty-four-hour donut and coffee shop and Winchester Ridge was no exception. He picked out a couple of dozen assorted donuts along with a large coffee and an orange juice.

He returned to the apartment building just as dawn was breaking. Funny, this wasn't how he usually spent early mornings. He'd never shared breakfast with an expectant mother, either. With his offerings in hand, he returned to Mia's apartment and gave a loud knock before he walked in.

"It's me, Ms. Saunders. I've got something for you." After hearing Mia's greeting he walked into the bedroom.

She was still working on the computer. "I thought you went back to bed."

"Not after you talked about donuts." He raised the box. "Freshly made." He opened the large box and the aroma filled the room.

Mia groaned. "Oh, my God." She put the laptop aside and reached for one. He pulled back.

"I thought you were going to fight me for one."

She looked confused.

"Of course, if we were on a first-name basis, I'd happily share. Especially if someone had been willing to get up before dawn and help out a neighbor."

Mia was embarrassed by her actions. Yesterday after Jarrett had left, Nola had returned and told her how he'd stayed at the hospital and called everyone with any news. She was even more ashamed when she learned that he'd bought the paint for her bedroom.

"It does seem to be one-sided, doesn't it? I apologize. You have helped me so much. I don't know how I would have made it to the hospital without you."

"Did I say I minded helping you? I just don't want to keep being treated like the enemy here. I can't change things that happened in the past."

"I know. I'm sorry, Jarrett."

He smiled. "What did you say?"

She sighed. He wasn't going to make this easy. "Would you be my friend, Jarrett?"

"You just want my donuts."

She nodded. "And you'd be wise not to get between a pregnant woman and those donuts."

He put the box down and her mouth watered as she eyed the selections. "There are so many to choose from." She rubbed her stomach, feeling the baby kicking her.

He sat at the end of the bed. "Are you all right?" he asked as he nodded to her stomach.

"Yeah, he's just active and hungry."

"Does he move around like that all the time?"

"Well, the baby's bigger now, so I feel it more."

He handed her juice. "Here's something to wash down your donut."

"Thank you." She motioned to the box. "Aren't you going to have one, too?"

"Sure, but ladies first."

"Wise choice." She couldn't help but smile as she bit into the jelly-filled treat. "Mmm, it's so good."

"You might not be able to have caffeine, but you're definitely getting a sugar rush."

Mia watched Jarrett finish off a glazed donut in record time. He looked good even with his finger-combed hair and wrinkled clothes. There were just some men who couldn't look bad. He was one of them.

"I should let you rest." He stood, but his gaze

never left hers. "Is there anything you need me to do before I go?"

She hesitated to ask him anything else.

"Come on, Mia. What is it?"

"I can wait for Nola."

"What for?"

"I need to take a shower, but the doctor said someone should be close by." She waved her hand. "Don't worry about it, Nola's coming in a few hours."

He swallowed. "How close by?"

"Just in the apartment. In case something happens there'll be someone to help me."

He stood there for what seemed like forever, and then he said, "Sure, what are friends for?"

Once Jarrett heard the shower go on, he took out his cell phone and began to check his messages. He had to get some things done today. One was to stop by the office for a few hours and check in with his agents.

Over the last couple of days, between the repairs here and keeping watch on one pregnant lady, he'd neglected his other business.

He was surprised at the next message. It was from Carrie Johnston. He smiled. The pretty blonde from Glenwood Springs he'd met at the real estate conference in Denver last summer had left him another suggestive message. She wanted to see him.

Jarrett should feel a little more excited. During their time together, the two had definitely set off sparks. So why wasn't he more interested in her invitation?

When it came to women, he'd always loved having variety in his life. So why suddenly did it seem too much trouble to make the effort? Maybe thirty-seven was too old to keep playing games.

He thought about what Mia had said, *You look it.*

He wasn't *that* old. Wasn't he considered in his prime? Okay, so most men were married by now, like his younger brother. Trace had found Kira years ago. And it had been love at first sight.

Jarrett didn't believe in that. He wasn't sure he believed in love at all.

Suddenly the bathroom door opened and Mia stepped out. She was dressed in her black stretch pants and a soft-pink sweater. Her dark hair lay against her shoulders in waves. Those big blue eyes looked at him and it became difficult to breathe. Damn. What was wrong with him? This woman came with far too many complications.

"Well, since you're finished, I'll go."

"Of course." She sat down on the sofa. "I appreciate you helping me. Thank you, Jarrett."

"Just do what the doctor told you and stay in bed. He pulled out his wallet and handed her his business card. "If you need anything."

She nodded.

"I mean it. Don't be stubborn about asking for help." He found he wanted to be the one she called.

The snow had been coming down like a holiday greeting card, but by the next afternoon, Mia was getting cabin fever.

She had watched every television talk show and finished up her work on the computer, even cried over an old movie. Neighbors stopped by with offers of help. Even parishioners from her brother's church had called her. She'd taken naps off and on for the past two days and she was still exhausted and totally bored. And no Jarrett.

"You know next week is Thanksgiving." Nola's voice broke through her reverie. "And we have a problem. The oven in the community room is broken."

"You can use mine. It's a little tricky on the temperature, but we could adjust it. It's small though. Don't we usually cook three or four turkeys?"

The older woman nodded. "Remember last

year we fed those people from the mission? There were nearly fifty here."

Mia thought back to last year. She'd had family then. Brad and Karen had just begun to research surrogacy as an alternative for a baby. And by Christmas, Mia had volunteered to carry her brother and his wife's child. They all were so happy, and then in a flash she had lost them both.

Tears flooded Mia's eyes and she quickly brushed them away. She looked at Nola. "I'm sorry."

Her friend sat down beside her. "There's no reason to be sorry, dear. We all miss Brad and Karen. They were wonderful people, but they left you a child. A child you get to love and raise as your own. What a special gift."

"I do know. And I love this baby, but I'm scared. What if I can't be a good mother?"

"I have no doubt you'll be a wonderful mother. You know why? Because you're a wonderful person and this little boy or girl will be blessed to have you."

"Oh, Nola. I hope you're right."

"I am. You know what else? We're all going to be around to help you."

She cleared her throat. "I'm so glad because I'm going to need you."

Nola patted her hand. "Well, count on me.

Now that that is settled, where are we going to find a big enough oven to cook our Thanksgiving Day turkeys? The ones at the church are already being used, and ours barely work. Too bad Jarrett couldn't replace the one in the community center."

"I'm not going to do that," a familiar voice said, "But I may have another solution."

Jarrett hadn't meant to eavesdrop, but he'd wanted to check on Mia and had found the door partly open.

"I overheard. You're having trouble finding working ovens."

Nodding, Nola stood. "We always feed a large group on Thanksgiving. And this might be the last one that we're all together." Her eyes brightened with tears. "You said you might have a solution."

"I have two large ovens at my house."

Nola immediately smiled. "You do?"

Jarrett stole a glance at Mia. She didn't look impressed by his offer. "Yes. When I built the house I was told it would be a good selling feature. They're like new." He shrugged. "You're welcome to them."

"Oh, my, that's the answer to our prayer." The older woman paused. "There's one condition. You have to come to our Thanksgiving celebration."

In the past Jarrett been happier to stay at home and watch football. He had gone by his brother's house last year for dessert, only because little Jenna had asked him to. He had a weakness for pretty young women. He glanced at Mia. Maybe is it was time to count some blessings. "I'd be honored to come by."

CHAPTER FIVE

HE had to be crazy to have suggested cooking Thanksgiving dinner here.

Jarrett stood back and watched as half a dozen women scurried around his kitchen. He'd told himself earlier that he wasn't going to hang around, but they'd showed up at dawn, ready and eager to begin the baking and cooking.

He had to admit that the place was filled with wonderful aromas. The one disappointment was that Mia wasn't there. It was crazy of him even to think about her at all. She was pregnant, and her life was going in one direction while he needed only to think about one thing—the computer-chip-factory project. And getting out of the jail of his crummy apartment.

Nola walked over to him. "You have a wonderful kitchen, Jarrett. Every modern convenience a woman could ever want. Seems such a waste that you don't have someone to share this with."

Jarrett smiled, but ignored her comment. "I'm glad you like it."

"Just so you know, we'll clean up everything. You won't even know we were here."

"I'm not worried. I have a cleaning service."

"Well, just the same. The place will be spotless when we leave."

Just then his phone rang. He grabbed the extension in the office. It was his brother. "Hi, Trace. Happy Thanksgiving."

"Same to you," Trace echoed. "I've been given orders to call you and see if you changed your mind about coming to dinner today."

Kira couldn't stand for him to be alone. "I appreciate the invitation, bro, but I seem to have a place to go. A few of the tenants have asked me to share the meal with them."

There was a long silence. "You better be careful, no telling what they might put in your food."

"Very funny. I do have a few friends. Besides, the tenants and I are getting along fine."

"Well, that's good."

He didn't want to talk about any apartment troubles. "I take it Kira is fixing dinner today."

"It'll be just us since Jody and Nathan have gone to be with Ben at the army base."

Jarrett remembered Kira's student who'd

gotten pregnant in high school. Jody had had the child and Ben had joined the military, but he'd stayed in touch. The couple had gotten married this past summer.

Suddenly the doorbell rang. "I've got to go, Trace. Tell everyone happy Thanksgiving."

After replacing the phone, Jarrett walked across the great room and into the entry. He pulled open the door to find Mia and several other people standing on his porch.

He frowned. "What are you doing out of bed?"

"I'm allowed out now. Some," she added stubbornly. "I just have to stay off my feet as much as possible."

He took her by the arm and led her to the sofa, followed by the other dozen or so tenants. "Why did you come here? We're going to bring the food back to the community room." He folded his arms. "You aren't supposed to do anything."

She nodded. I know, but there's a problem at the community room. It's flooded."

Jarrett cursed. He didn't need another thing that he had to pay for. "How bad?"

Joe spoke up. "I shut off the main valve, but there's about an inch of water on the floor."

Jarrett murmured some choice words as he turned back to Mia.

She suddenly looked unsure. "We didn't know what to do, so we came here."

Nola walked into the room. "Mia, what's wrong? Is it the baby?"

"No, I'm fine, but the community room is flooded." Mia looked back at Jarrett. "We have no place to have our dinner."

Every eye turned toward him. He had no choice. "Well, since everyone is here, I guess it'll be at my house."

Cheers filled the room, then everyone scattered to do their chores. He pulled out his phone and punched in the McKane Ranch number, wondering how he'd gotten into this situation. He glanced at Mia Saunders, those big blue eyes staring back at him. A sudden stirring in his gut told him he was headed for disaster if he wasn't careful. Hell, he'd never been careful in his life.

His brother answered the phone.

"Hey, Trace. Why don't you load up Kira and Jenna and come here? It seems I'm having Thanksgiving at my house."

Two hours later, Mia was still sitting on the large sofa in Jarrett's great room. Although it wasn't her taste, the place was decorated well. A lot of chrome-and-glass tables and black leather furniture filled the room. The most beautiful feature was the huge wall of windows and the French door that led to the deck and the wooded area at the back of the house. Although the trees were bare and a dusting of snow covered the ground, she could picture it in the spring with green trees and wildflowers along the hillside.

She turned toward the open-concept kitchen, looking over the breakfast bar to see rows of espresso-colored cabinets, and marble counter tops. The commercial-size stainless-steel appliances looked as though they were getting a rare workout today.

The dining room was on the other side, the long table already set up for the meal, along with several card tables scattered around to accommodate all the people coming today. Mia didn't even want to count them. All she knew was that her brother and sister-in-law wouldn't be at any table. These people were her family now. She rubbed her stomach. Hers and her baby's.

"Are you okay?"

She glanced up to see Jarrett standing beside the sofa. "I'm fine. Really. Thank you for having us today."

"There wasn't a choice, and you know it."

"It's still very generous that you let us use your home."

He shrugged. "I also get a home-cooked meal."

"You have family. And I bet you could get someone to cook for you pretty easily."

His dark gaze held hers. "I'm pretty selective in choosing my friends." His mouth crooked upward in a sexy smile. "Also who cooks for me."

"Well, you've got some pretty good cooks in your kitchen right now."

"I'm glad about that, because I'm getting hungry just smelling all the wonderful aromas." He sat down across from her. "If your cookies are any indication, I'd say you know your way around a kitchen, too."

The man was too handsome and, when he wanted to be, charming. She scooted to the edge of the sofa. "Could you direct me to the bathroom, please?"

"Of course." He helped her up, but didn't release his hold on her arm. They were walking toward the hall when the doorbell rang.

She looked at him. "I thought everyone was here."

Jarrett pulled open the door to a young couple with a little girl. She recognized them from church.

"Happy Thanksgiving, Unca Jay," the girl cried as she ran inside.

He scooped her into his arms. "Happy

Thanksgiving to you too, Jenna. I'm glad you could come today. Welcome, Kira, Trace."

They all exchanged greetings.

Jenna kept her hold on her uncle. "Mama said it must be a really special day because we never get invited to your house. She's really happy because family should be together."

"Jenna," her mother warned.

"Well, you did say that," the child acknowledged, then looked at Mia. "Who's this lady, Unca Jay?"

"Hi, I'm Mia."

Jarrett set her down. "I'm Jenna, and I'm almost four years old. But my daddy says I'm really thirty." The child caught sight of Mia's rounded stomach. "Are you going to have a baby?"

"Jenna." Kira sent another warning glance to her daughter, and then looked at Mia. "Hi, Mia. It's good to see you again."

Trace removed his cowboy hat and nodded. "Hello, Mia."

"Nice to see you, too. I hope you don't mind that we took over Jarrett's house."

The pretty blonde smiled and glanced up at her husband. Love radiated between them just as Mia had seen between her brother and his wife.

"We think it's wonderful," Kira said. "I'm just wondering how you did it."

"I believe a judge did it, along with several of the tenants."

They all looked toward the living room and saw the numerous people. "Welcome to Mountain View Apartment's Thanksgiving Day celebration." Mia turned to Kira. "If you'll excuse me, I need to find a restroom."

Jarrett watched Mia walk down the hall. He wanted to go after her. Why? She was capable of finding the bathroom.

"How is she doing?"

Jarrett looked at his sister-in-law. "She should be off her feet. So would you watch her?"

"Sure. If you and Trace unload the car. I brought a few things for dinner, too. I'll take Jenna to the kitchen and see if they need any help."

"Just ask for Nola."

"I know Nola Madison. I see her at church nearly every week."

"Okay. You'll probably know a few of the others, too."

Once the group of seniors spotted Jenna, they began to fuss over her. His niece couldn't get enough of the attention.

"So tell me about you and Mia Saunders," Trace said.

Jarrett turned around. "There's nothing to tell. She had a scare with her pregnancy and I had to take her to the hospital. The doctor ordered bed rest. She was allowed to come here, but she needs to stay off her feet."

He glanced down the hall. "And if she doesn't come out soon, I'm going in to get her."

Trace arched an eyebrow. "So when did you become her protector?"

Jarrett turned to his younger half brother. Trace stared back at him.

"She doesn't have anyone else," Jarrett reminded him. "Remember, she lost her brother a few months back."

Trace nodded. "Yeah, Reverend Brad was a good man," he said, studying Jarrett. "I just never knew my brother to care much about anything that wasn't about the almighty dollar. You must be getting soft in your old age."

"Hey, I'm not that old." He didn't want to discuss his age or his relationship with Mia. They were neighbors. Temporary neighbors. "But don't go thinking I've bought into the family scene."

"Never say never, bro," Trace challenged. "I've seen you with Jenna. You wouldn't be a bad dad."

Jarrett froze. He didn't want to be a dad at all. His own father had been lousy at the job. "Look, as soon as I make the repairs to the complex, I'm out of there. And I won't be looking back."

* * *

On returning from the bathroom, Mia discovered that everyone was taking a seat at the tables. She glanced around for to find one last vacant chair. Next to Jarrett.

Smiling, he stood and pulled out her chair. "Looks like you're next to me."

She caught Nola smiling from across the table. Little Jenna was on the other side of Jarrett and Trace and Kira sat beside her. "I'm just happy we have a place to eat. Thank you, Jarrett, for having us here."

Nola and Margaret stood and went into the kitchen and soon returned, each woman carrying a platter with a large turkey. The group made approving sounds as the birds were placed on the table alongside sweet potatoes, green-bean casseroles, stuffing, gravy and other side dishes too numerous to count.

Nola stood beside the table. "Before we all dig in, we should give thanks for this wonderful day." She turned to Jarrett.

Mia watched as he nudged his brother and said something to him. Trace nodded. "Everyone, take hands and let's bow our heads."

Jarrett reached for Mia's hand. His large palm nearly engulfed hers. She was surprised by the roughness of his fingers, but also by the warmth he generated.

"Dear Lord," Trace began. "We thank you

for all the blessings you've given us this past year. There have been some rough times, but sometimes that brings out the best in people. And today, we see that special bond as friends gather together as a family.

"We also ask for your blessing for those who aren't here with us." Trace paused. Mia thought about Brad and Karen. She felt Jarrett squeeze her hand. "We also ask a special blessing for Mia's baby.

"We ask you to bless this food in your name. Amen."

"Amens" echoed around the room.

Mia kept her head lowered, thinking of her brother and his wife. How much she missed them. Brad had always been there to guide her, to spout optimism whenever she wanted to give up. Now, she had to go on without him.

She opened her eyes to see that she was still holding hands with Jarrett. She turned to him to catch him watching her.

"Are you okay?" he asked.

"I'm fine." She pulled her hand away. "I wish people would stop asking me that."

"Then eat a good meal today, and we'll get you home to bed."

His deep voice caused her to shiver. "I can get myself to bed, thank you," she said in a quiet voice.

"Well, one thing is for sure, you're not climbing the steps."

Since when did he become the boss of her? "I wouldn't have to if you'd fix the elevator."

He glared. "That will be Monday. I can't get anyone out before then."

She heard his name called and they both looked up at Nola.

"Jarrett and Trace, would you do the honor of slicing the turkeys?"

The brothers stood, went to opposite ends of the table and began to carve. The side dishes were passed around and Mia put small helpings onto her plate. With Jarrett gone, she dished up food for him, too.

"Are you Unca Jay's girlfriend?" Jenna McKane asked from across her uncle's empty seat.

Mia smiled. "No. We're neighbors in his apartment building in town."

The little girl frowned and turned to her mother. "Mommy, what's an apartment?"

"It's a big building with a lot of houses inside. It's like where Aunt Michele lives."

"Oh." The child turned back to Mia's stomach. "Are you going to have a baby soon?"

"Yes, I am, in just a few weeks."

Jenna grinned. "I have a big brother, Jack. He's old and he doesn't live with us. So my mommy and daddy are trying to have a brother or sister for me."

"Jenna McKane," Kira said, giving her daughter a stern look. "You don't have to talk so much. Now, eat."

Kira looked at Mia. "I'm sorry. Trace and I forget how much she hears."

Mia smiled as the platter of turkey was passed to her. She nodded toward the child eating mashed potatoes. "She's adorable."

Kira looked at her daughter lovingly. "She's our miracle baby. And a very welcome surprise." She looked at Mia. "If you ever need anything, Mia, please don't hesitate to ask. All of us in the church want very much to help."

Mia was touched. "Thank you, Kira. Everyone has been so generous already. I think I'll be fine if I can find a place to live by spring."

Before Kira could say any more, Jarrett arrived back in his seat. For the next twenty minutes everyone concentrated on the delicious food and friendly conversation. Finally the men leaned back groaning at the amount of food they'd consumed.

"There's pie, too," Nola announced as she stood and took several empty plates. She looked at Jarrett. "Jarrett, would you mind helping me with the coffeemaker? I'm not sure on the measurements."

With a nod, he stood. "Sure." He grinned. "If I get first choice of pie."

Nola smiled, too. "You think because you're good-looking, you can charm me into anything, don't you?"

"Hey, I do what I can to get an advantage." He put his arm around her shoulders. "Is it working?"

Mia never heard the answer as they walked off together.

"He's a flirt, but he's a good man."

Mia turned to Kira, but didn't know how to answer that. Was Kira trying to sell her brother-in-law's better qualities to her?

"I wouldn't have said that a few years ago," Kira went on. "But something in him has changed. And he and Trace are working on being brothers."

She turned and looked at Mia. "I know you're not happy about having to leave your apartment, but I might be able to help with that. We have a guest house at the ranch. It's small, but it has two bedrooms. A friend had been living there during college, and now she's gone to be with her husband in the army."

"Oh, Kira." Mia didn't want to get too excited. "What about Trace? I bet you haven't even asked him."

"Haven't asked me what?" her husband turned toward her.

"About Mia coming to live in the cottage."

He raised an eyebrow as if to think about it. "That's a great idea. The house is sitting empty." He shrugged. "You're welcome to live there as long as you need."

Mia was getting excited. "What is the rent?"

"There isn't any rent."

"No, I would expect to pay something."

Trace glanced at his wife. "I think we owe your brother a bigger debt. He helped us through some rough spots a few years ago. I think Brad would want us to help you and the baby."

"Can I come over to see the baby?" Jenna asked. "I'll be really quiet."

"If I decide to move there, of course, you can." She looked at Kira. "Maybe I could even babysit you so your parents could go out."

A big smile split Trace's face. "That's a deal I'll take."

"What's a deal?" Jarrett sat down next to Mia.

Trace was still smiling. "Mia is coming to live in the guest house at the ranch."

"The hell she is."

* * *

The entire room went silent at his outburst.

"Unca Jay, you said a bad word," Jenna piped in.

Jarrett reached into his pocket, pulled out change and set it on the table for his misstep. "Here, sweetie." Then he turned to Mia. "You can't move all the way out there. Not in the winter."

She glanced around nervously. "I don't want to talk about this now," she said as she pushed away from the table. "Excuse me." She stood and walked out.

Jarrett went after her. He caught up with her right before she got to the bathroom door. She would have disappeared, but someone was using the facility.

"Mia," he called.

"Go away."

"That's not likely." He gripped her by the arm and escorted her down the hall.

"What are you doing?"

"Taking you to a bathroom."

"I don't have to go. I just needed to get away from you and your crazy idea that you can tell me what to do."

He wasn't listening as he took her by the hand, led her to the master suite and opened the door to the large room. He pulled her inside and shut the door.

"Stop this," she demanded. "And stop telling me what to do. You can't boss me around."

He glared at her. "Someone needs to take you in hand. You can't move all the way out to the ranch. If we get a snowstorm—and the possibility is strong that we will—you might not make it to the hospital when the time comes."

"I can take care of myself. And why does it matter to you, anyway? You are my landlord, Mr. McKane, not my keeper."

"Dammit, stop calling me that. It's Jarrett." He leaned closer as her eyes widened. "Say *Jarrett*."

"Jarrett…"

His gaze moved to her full lips. Suddenly, he ached to know how they would feel against his and how she would taste. He couldn't resist and slowly lowered his mouth to hers. He took a gentle bite, then another. Each one a little sweeter than the last.

Her eyes widened, her breathing grew labored.

Finally, he closed his mouth over hers and wasn't disappointed. With a groan, he wrapped his arms around her and drew her closer. She made a whimpering sound and her arms move to around his neck as he deepened the kiss.

Jarrett pressed her back against the door, feeling her body against his, then suddenly something kicked against his stomach. The baby. He broke off the kiss with a gasp, suddenly remembering the situation.

Mia's shocked gaze searched his. "Why did you do that?"

"Hell if I know." He hated that he was so drawn to her. She was a complication he didn't need, but he couldn't seem to stay away from her.

Her hand went to her stomach protectively. Was she having a contraction?

He picked her up in his arms and carried her across the room.

"What are you doing?" she demanded.

"Taking you where you should have been in the first place. To bed."

CHAPTER SIX

MIA was fuming as Jarrett walked out the door, leaving her alone on the bed. His bed. What she hated the most was that she didn't have much say in the matter.

All her life, she'd had to do what she'd been told. Go to the best schools, make the best grades, be the perfect daughter. It had taken years, and although she'd made many bad turns she'd finally gained her independence. She wasn't about to give it up now. Not even for a man.

She glanced around Jarrett's bedroom. Large, dark furniture dominated the spacious room, including the king-size bed with the carved headboard. The walls were a taupe-gray and the floors a wide-planked dark wood. Two honey-colored leather chairs sat in front of huge French doors that led out to a deck and the wooded area beyond. It was definitely a man's room, which reminded her she shouldn't be in here.

Mia's thoughts turned back to Jarrett McKane.

What had possessed her to let him kiss her? She shut her eyes reliving the feel of his mouth against hers, his strong arms around her. What she hadn't expected was the way she had reacted to him.

Of course, she would react to the man—any man for that matter. How long had it been since she'd been in a relationship? She couldn't even remember that far back. Not that she was eager to start one now. There hadn't been any time for a man. Then Mr. Hotshot McKane had stormed into her life, with his good looks and his take-charge attitude. No, she didn't need him in her life.

She started to get up when she felt the mild contraction and covered her midsection with her hand.

"Oh, please, no."

After several slow, relaxing breaths she eased back against the pillows and shut her eyes. Why had she come here today? Okay, she'd wanted to come to the party. And Dr. Drake had said she could be out for a few hours if she was careful and didn't overdo things.

Mia caressed her stomach, feeling the tension slowly ease from her body.

There was a soft knock and the door opened and Jarrett came in carrying a tray with a slice of pie. He stopped at the side of the bed, frowning. "You okay?"

"I'm fine," she fibbed. "I'm just resting."

He continued to stare at her. "You don't look fine."

She closed her eyes again. "Then don't look at me."

He sat the plate on the nightstand. "Are you having contractions?"

She opened her eyes. "Just a little one."

Jarrett pulled out his wallet from his back pocket and took out a business card. He grabbed the phone off the table.

"What are you doing?" she asked.

"Calling your doctor."

"You can't, it's Thanksgiving."

"Then we go to the emergency room." He paused. "Your choice."

Jarrett had worried this might happen if Mia left the apartment. They were lucky that Dr. Drake was on call today, and it only took her minutes to return his call.

The doctor talked with Mia, who didn't look happy when she handed the phone back to Jarrett.

"Yes, Doctor?" he said.

"I instructed Mia not to get out of bed for anything except to use the bathroom, and I want her in my office first thing in the morning. Could you bring her in?"

"We'll be there when your doors open." He ended the call and hung up. "Looks like you'll be staying here tonight."

He watched her eyes widen. "I can't stay here. It's not fair to you."

"Hey, I haven't been staying here anyway."

"But this is your room, your bed."

Smiling, he glanced around at the large space. "I guess we'll have to share."

She glared. "You need to get a life, McKane."

"I have a life, thank you, or at least I did before I moved into the Mountain View Apartments."

There was another soft knock on the door and Kira peered in. "Is everything okay?" she asked.

"It's under control now. Mia's had some contractions. Her doctor wants her to stay in bed and come in tomorrow."

Mia sat up. "I tried to tell Jarrett that I'll be able to rest better in my own apartment."

Kira stood at the end of the bed. "I know this is difficult, Mia, but you really need to stay put. In the last months when I was pregnant with Jenna, I couldn't even sit up to eat."

"See," Jarrett said. "And she delivered a healthy baby. So you stay."

Suddenly two more people appeared at the door, Nola and Sylvia, looking concerned.

"Please don't worry," Mia said. "I'm fine. But I guess I have to stay put for tonight."

Nola came closer and patted her hand. "We're not worried. Jarrett will take care of you." She looked down at the tray of food. "You need to eat."

Jarrett backed out of the room, leaving the women to pamper Mia. He couldn't help but wonder if he was the cause of her problem.

He rubbed his hand over his face. He had no business near her, let alone kissing her.

What happened to keeping your distance, McKane? The woman is pregnant, for Christ's sake.

He looked up to see Trace coming down the hall. "Is everything okay?"

Hell, would the cavalry be coming next? "Mia had a few contractions, but she's resting now."

"That's good." Trace studied him. "You seem to have inherited a lot more than just an apartment building. Need any help?"

Jarrett wasn't surprised at his brother's offer. For years the kid had tried to get close to him, but Jarrett had always rebuffed him. It made him ashamed of his past actions.

"Thanks, but I'm handling it."

Trace smiled. "I never thought I'd see the day

my brother entertained a group of senior citizens in his house and had a pregnant woman in his bed."

Jarrett started to argue, but he had no words.

Trace grinned. "Be careful, bro, you're getting soft, or else, Mia Saunders is doing something no other woman ever has."

Jarrett sighed. "I don't want to hear this." He walked out into the great room, seeing the rest of his guests waiting for some news. He hoped he could convince them everything would be okay. First he had to convince himself.

Darkness surrounded her, but Mia knew she wasn't alone. The small room was filled with loud music, a lot of voices trying to be heard. She could smell cigarette smoke. Someone was smoking.

No! It was bad for the baby. She tried to stand, but someone pulled her back down.

"You can't leave, honey," a man with a slurred voice said. "The party's only getting started. Here have another drink." He put a glass in front of her face and she nearly gagged on the stale smell of beer.

"No! Let me go." She managed to break his hold, and get out the door. The night's cold air caused her to shiver as she looked around, but

she couldn't recognize anything. She had no idea where she was, but knew she had to get home. But she had no home.

"Margaret!"

She turned and saw her father. She gasped and tried to run, but her legs were too heavy to move fast and Preston Saunders grabbed her arm.

"You can't get away from me," he threatened.

"Let me go," she cried. "I don't want you."

"I don't want you either, but my grandchild is a different matter. If you think I'll let you raise this baby you'd better think again. It's a Saunders."

"No, it's my baby. It's mine! It's mine!" she cried.

"Mia! Mia! Wake up."

She felt another touch. This time it was different. Gentler. Soothing. She opened her eyes and saw Jarrett leaning over her. With a gasp she went into his arms and held on. Tight.

Jarrett felt her trembling. His arms circled her back and pulled her close and he felt her breasts pressed against his bare chest. The awareness shook him, but he worked to ease her fears.

"Ssh, you were having a bad dream. It's okay, Mia." He felt her tears against his shoulder. "I'm here."

She shivered again and then pulled back but refused to look at him. "I'm sorry."

With the moonlight coming through the French doors, he could see she wasn't all right.

"Bad dream, huh? You want to tell me about it?"

She shook her head, but didn't let go of his hand. "It's just one of those where someone is chasing you."

"Anyone you know?"

She shrugged. "Just someone from a long time ago."

That had him wondering about a lot of things. "A bad-news ex-boyfriend?"

She didn't answer for a long time. He suddenly became aware she was wearing one of his T-shirts, and he was only in a pair of sweatpants, all cozy together on his bed.

"I don't want to talk about it."

He nodded. "Do you want me to get you anything?"

She shook her head. "No, thank you."

"Should I leave?"

She finally looked at him. "Would you mind staying? For a little while?"

He had to hide his surprise. He didn't cuddle with women, not unless it led to something. He was about say, "Not a good idea," but instead he answered, "Not a problem." He changed position, propping himself against the headboard and pulled her back into his arms. "This okay?"

She nodded and then lay back down, her head against her pillow next to him. She blinked up at him with those trusting eyes.

Okay, this wasn't going to work. "Try and get some sleep."

"I don't want to start dreaming again."

He covered her hand with his. "I'm here, Mia. No one will hurt you or your baby as long as I'm around."

Somehow she'd managed to get to him, and he'd just taken on the job of her protector. It was crazy, but he didn't mind one bit.

Mia snuggled deeper into the warmth, enjoying the comfort of the soft bed. She smiled, feeling the strong arms that were wrapped around her back, holding her close.

Slowly, memories of last night began drifting back to her. The nightmare. Her father.

She opened her eyes and was greeted by bright sunlight coming through the French doors. What was more disturbing was the feeling of the bare skin against her cheek. She raised her head to see she was in bed with Jarrett McKane.

Oh, God. What was he still doing here?

She studied the sleeping man who was making

soft snoring sounds. He suddenly turned toward her, reaching for her, pulling her against him.

Oh no. His chest was hard and doing incredible things to her out-of-whack libido. But she had a more desperate urge right now. She had to use the bathroom, and quick.

Careful not to disturb him, Mia managed to untangle herself, slide to the side of the bed and escape into the connecting bath.

A few minutes later she returned to find Jarrett awake and leaning against the headboard. His chest was gloriously naked, exposing every defined muscle under his bronzed skin.

"Morning," he murmured, raking fingers through his hair. "We seem to make a habit of this."

She had to put a stop to it. "Well, as soon as I get back to my apartment I won't be bothering you anymore."

Frowning, he got up and came around to her. "First thing, you need to get back into bed," he told her, giving her a little nudge to climb in. Once she complied, he continued, "Secondly, I wasn't complaining, just stating a fact."

Jarrett hadn't had much time for female companionship the past few months. Lately it had all been about business, until Mia Saunders and her group of merry followers had appeared in his life. They might be a costly headache, but he'd found he liked the diversion.

He sat on the edge of the bed. His gaze moved over her soft brunette curls and met her pretty blue eyes. Damn, he could get used to this. "Any more dreams?" He could still hear her frightened cries.

She shook her head. "I slept fine. Thank you."

He smiled and finally coaxed one from her. *Damn, she's pretty,* he thought, suddenly realizing his body was noticing, too.

"Okay, I better get breakfast started." He stood. "Will you eat eggs, or do I need to go on a jelly-donut run?"

Two hours later, Mia sat in the exam room with Doctor Drake, with Jarrett sitting just outside.

After the exam, the doctor pulled off her gloves. "You're doing fine."

"What does *fine* mean?" Mia asked as she sat up.

"You're effaced fifty percent."

"Oh, God. Am I going into labor?"

She shook her head. "You aren't dilated yet. And you haven't had any more contractions, right?"

"Not since last night."

There was a knock on the door and a technician came in pushing a machine.

"I want to do an ultrasound as a precaution," the doctor explained.

"So you are worried?" Mia asked.

"A little concerned. This baby coming early is a very real possibility." She raised a calming hand. "You're thirty-six weeks, Mia. All I want to do is check the baby's weight."

There was a knock on the door. "Yes?" the doctor called.

Jarrett poked his head in. "Is everything okay?"

The doctor glanced at Mia. "You want him in here?"

Mia looked at Jarrett and found herself nodding. "You can stay if you want," she told him.

He looked surprised but walked right toward her as she lay back on the table. Although covered with a paper sheet, she realized that she'd be exposing her belly for Jarrett to see.

Dr. Drake nodded toward the opposite side of the exam table for Jarrett to stand, then she began to apply the clear gel on her stomach.

Mia sucked in a breath.

Jarrett took her hand. "You okay?"

She nodded. "The cream is cold."

The doctor went to the machine and made

some adjustments, then began to move the probe over her stomach.

Jarrett had no idea what he was doing here. Then he saw Mia's fear, and knew he couldn't leave her. He eyed the machine, watching the grainy picture, and then suddenly it came into focus. He saw a head first, then a small body.

"Well, I'll be damned," he murmured, seeing the incredible image. "That's a baby."

"What did you think it was?" the doctor chided.

Jarrett was embarrassed. "The way she's craved jelly donuts, I wasn't sure."

The doctor laughed. "Since your weight's okay, I'll tell you to indulge, a little. After the baby comes, you'll be on a stricter diet while you're breast-feeding." The doctor glanced at Mia, then back at the screen. "The baby's in position. So that's one less thing to worry about. This is a 3D machine so let's get a better look at this little one." The picture became a lot clearer and a tiny face appeared.

"Oh, my gosh," Mia cried and gripped Jarrett's hand tighter. "It's crazy but he looks like Brad's baby pictures." Tears formed in her eyes and a sob came out. "I'm sorry."

The doctor patted her arm. "It's understand-able. Are you ready to know the sex?"

Mia looked at Jarrett. He shrugged, trying to handle his own emotions. "I say it's a boy."

Mia gave a slight nod and the doctor scanned in for a closer look. He saw all the proof he needed. "Well, hello, BJ."

Mia gave him a questioning look.

"I take it you're naming this little guy after your brother," he said. "Bradley Junior."

During the ride home from Grand Junction, Mia had zoned out, not noticing much of the trip until Jarrett stopped in front of the apartment building.

"We're home," he said, but didn't move to get out of the car. "Mia, are you all right?"

No! she wanted to scream. She hadn't been okay since the day her brother had died. She looked at Jarrett, seeing his concern. "Seeing the baby today made it seem so real." Her voice grew softer, more hoarse. "A boy. How can I raise a boy?" Tears filled her eyes, but she couldn't cry any more. "A boy needs a father. Brad should be here."

He reached across the console and took her hand. Even with the heater going, her hands were still cold. "Hey, this kid's got the next best thing. You."

She wasn't the best. "You don't know that. I've done things, made bad choices."

"I can't believe that, or your brother wouldn't have chosen you to carry this baby."

"But not to raise his son." She sighed. "Besides, I've always had Brad to help me, to guide me in life. Now, I'm on my own. What if I make mistakes again?"

He frowned. "Everyone makes mistakes, Mia, but you can't just give up."

Jarrett had never been the optimistic type, but he was a good salesman. "Don't forget, you have friends to help you. Is there any other family around?"

Mia shook her head. "No. There's no one else." She wiped her eyes. "God, I hate this. I never cry."

"I hear it's normal," he consoled her, hating that he kept getting more and more involved in her life. Not to mention the lives of the other tenants, too.

Once he got off house arrest and they all found other places to live, this time would just be a fleeting memory. They wouldn't be his problem then. They'd move on, and he'd move on. But could he? He thought back to being beside Mia and seeing her baby on the ultrasound.

Damn. He needed to get this apartment building in shape and get the hell out of here. "We'd better get inside and out of the cold so you can rest."

She grumbled. "That's all I've been doing."

"From what Kira tells me you won't get much sleep after the baby comes, so enjoy it now." He started to climb out of the car when she stopped him with a soft touch on his arm.

She nodded in agreement. "Thank you," she said softly. "Thank you for being there with me today."

He caught her pretty blue eyes still glistening with tears and something tightened in his chest. Dear Lord. He was in big trouble.

CHAPTER SEVEN

By the next week, Jarrett had accomplished several things. He'd finally gotten one of the elevators repaired and a plumber had replaced the rusted pipes in the community room. Somehow, he'd even been talked into helping put up some Christmas decorations. Joe convinced him that since this would be Mia's baby's first Christmas, they should celebrate it.

The major thing he'd wanted to do was keep his distance from Mia. He'd gotten too involved with the expectant mother.

Thanks to Nola, Jarrett knew how Mia was doing, whether he wanted to or not. By afternoon, he'd seen several women going into his neighbor's apartment carrying presents for a baby shower.

Kira and Jenna stopped by his place afterward to see him and tell him all about the gifts Mia had gotten for the baby. His niece also had several things to say about the condition of his temporary home. None were good.

"Unca Jay, I like your other house better."

"I still have my other house, sweetie. I'll move back there soon."

She smiled, then looked thoughtful. "But you have to take care of Mia until she has her baby. Promise you will."

What was going on? "Okay, I promise as long as I live here I'll watch out for Mia and the baby."

That seemed to satisfy the three-year-old and she smiled. "Then you can come see her at the ranch. She's going to move in with the new baby." She turned to her mother and was practically jumping up and down. "I can't wait. I get to hold the baby, too."

Jarrett looked at his sister-in-law. "So, it's definite?"

Kira nodded. "I'm pretty sure I have her convinced it's best for her and the child."

"Isn't that neat, Unca Jay, she's gonna be in our family? It's almost going to be our baby, too."

"That's great," he said.

The girl's eyes lit up more. "Maybe if you ask, Mia will share her baby with you, too."

Jarrett looked at Kira for help, hoping she didn't read anything more into his relationship with his neighbor. "Where does she get this stuff?"

Kira only smiled. "Sounds like a pretty good idea to me."

The next day Jarrett drove to his office, McKane Properties, and started two of his staff working on finding affordable apartments for some of the tenants. He needed to get this over and done with.

He needed everyone to move on, but if Mia and the baby moved out to the ranch, he'd still see her. Would that be so bad? With Kira and Trace looking out for her, at least he wouldn't worry about her so much.

That way he could go back to business as usual and a life without Mia in it. He turned his thoughts to the day at the doctor's office and seeing the ultrasound. He'd had no business sharing that with her. Just as he'd had no business kissing her Thanksgiving Day.

He had to stay away.

There were other things he needed to think about, like the Fulton plant project. It had been a big cause of his loss of sleep. He'd been working on some changes, changes to the factory site that might help everyone.

For him to survive financially, Jarrett knew he

had to finalize this deal, or he might be living in the Mountain View Apartments permanently.

A few days later Jarrett was awakened in the middle of the night by his ringing phone. He grabbed it off the bedside table.

"Hello," he groaned.

"Jarrett," a familiar voice said. "I'm sorry to bother you, but could you come over?"

"Sure." He hung up, got out of bed, pulled on jeans and shirt along with boots. He crossed the hall, but before he could knock she opened the door.

At 3:00 a.m. in the morning, she looked fresh and dressed for the day. Her dark hair lay in waves around her shoulders and she even had on makeup. "I take it the call wasn't for a donut run?" he joked.

"I need you to take me to the hospital. My water broke."

He froze, then his heart began to race. "You're in labor?"

She nodded. "I've only had some light contractions, but Doctor Drake said I need to come in now."

"Of course." He pointed to his apartment. "Let me grab my car keys." He rushed back, slipped on a coat and hurried back to find her waiting with a small bag.

"I hated to ask you, but Nola's daughter is sick and she's helping with the grandkids," Mia apologized.

He took her by the arm and they slowly made their way to the elevator. "I'm glad you asked me, I don't want Nola to drive at night." He gave her the once-over. "You okay?"

She smiled. "Outside of being a little scared, I feel pretty good."

"I think it's normal to feel scared."

They rode down one floor and the doors opened. "Thank you for helping me out, Jarrett. I know this isn't in your landlord duties."

"Hey, I told you it's not a problem." They stepped off the elevator and walked outside. "Is there anyone you want me to call?"

Mia shook her head. "Nola was supposed to be my coach, but I can't take her away from her grandkids."

"Is there a backup?"

She stopped and looked at him pleadingly. "You?"

"You're kidding?"

"Do you think I like asking you again?"

"I didn't say I mind doing it, I just don't know what to do." He wasn't making any sense.

"Join the club. This is my first time, too," she began, then suddenly groaned.

He saw the pain etched across her face, but it

was her fingernails digging into his arm that told him what was happening. Labor had begun.

"Looks like you're getting an early Christmas present."

Thirty minutes and five labor pains later, Jarrett pulled up at the emergency-room door. An attendant brought out a wheelchair, and Mia took the seat. Then Jarrett drove off and she was wheeled inside to get admitted.

After minimal paperwork, she was taken up to the maternity floor and into a labor/delivery room. Once dressed in a gown and in bed, she was hooked to monitors to watch her progress.

"Looks like you lose the bet for a Christmas-day baby."

Mia looked up as Dr. Drake walked in and nodded to the other doctor leaving. "December fifteenth seems like a fine birthday to me."

"How are you doing?" Lauren asked, checking the monitor.

No sooner were the words out than Mia felt a contraction begin to build.

"Breathe," the doctor instructed her as she came to the bedside. "It's almost over. There. Take a cleansing breath."

Mia sighed and lay back against the pillow. "That was stronger than the others."

"They're going to get even stronger before the

baby comes. Don't worry, the anesthesiologist should be here soon with your epidural." The doctor glanced around. "Do you have someone here with you?"

"Will I do?"

They both turned to find Jarrett standing in the doorway. He hadn't gone back home.

"Jarrett, you don't have to stay. This could take all night."

He came in anyway. "I called Kira and she's on her way. So how about I be a stand-in until she arrives?"

"Kira's coming all the way here?"

"I didn't ask her to, she just said she's coming to help you."

Mia had to blink back tears. She wasn't going to be alone. She managed a nod at Jarrett. "Thank you."

"I know my limitations. My only experience is birthing calves." He shook his head. "And that was a long time ago."

"I'd like to see you all decked out in Western gear, cowboy hat, chaps." Mia found herself saying, feeling oddly relaxed in between pains.

"Hey, I didn't look bad." She knew he was nervous about his role as coach and trying to distract her. "I had a few girls following me around when I did some rodeos. Calf-roping was my event. I was known for my quick hands."

Mia couldn't hide her smile. "I bet you were," she said as another contraction grabbed her. "Ooh…"

The doctor looked at Jarrett. "Do your job, coach," she told him.

Jarrett took Mia's hand as Lauren instructed him on what to do.

Over the next hour, Mia's contractions grew more frequent and more intense. It helped if she focused on Jarrett's encouraging words and gentle touch, even his humor. She did her breathing, and he wiped her brow.

After another series of strong contractions had eased, she noticed him watching her. She had to be a mess. Her hair was matted down and she was sweating as though she'd run a mile.

His dark eyes locked on hers. "You're amazing. And you haven't even complained once." He spooned her some ice chips that soothed her throat. "You're going to make a great mother."

"You're not doing so bad yourself. A great stand-in coach." She started to say more when the door opened and the anesthesiologist walked in.

It didn't take the doctor long to work his magic, and soon Mia was relaxed and feeling no discomfort, just pressure from the contractions.

Jarrett stood beside the bed. "Is it better now?"

Smiling, she nodded. "Isn't medication wonderful?"

He laughed. "I'd still have to be knocked out to go through what you're doing."

Over the next hour things began to move a lot faster. Mia's contractions started coming faster and harder, and they were different. She felt more pressure, lower.

Dr. Drake came in and checked the monitor. "Could you step outside a minute, Jarrett?"

He squeezed Mia's hand. "I'll be right back," he promised as he walked out.

The doctor checked her. "You're close, Mia," she told her. "It won't be long now."

"Really?" She glanced at the clock. She'd only been here a few hours.

Lauren smiled. "Sometimes it happens like this, short labor is rare with the first baby."

Mia's thoughts turned to Brad and Karen and sadness swamped her. They should have been here.

Outside the room, a nurse handed Jarrett some paper scrubs. "But I'm not her coach. My sister-in-law is supposed to be here."

The nurse frowned. "Well, if someone plans to be with her, they'd better get inside because she's ready to go."

Jarrett paused momentarily. He didn't want to leave Mia to do this alone. She hadn't complained, but there wasn't anyone else here. He quickly slipped on the scrubs and walked back into the room.

"If you want me to leave, I won't be offended. Just say the word."

Before Mia could speak a contraction seized her and she grabbed his hand. Things happened quickly after that. The doctor instructed him to stand behind Mia. He continued to coax her through each contraction, and held his breath with each push. When she became exhausted, he made her focus.

The next thing Jarrett knew he was witnessing a miracle as Mia's son made his noisy entrance into the world.

"Here's your son, Mia." Doctor Drake held the baby up for inspection.

Jarrett found he was counting fingers and toes and other male body parts. He swallowed hard. "Well, I don't think you're going to have any trouble hearing this guy."

He looked down to see Mia's tears. "He's so beautiful, don't you think?" she asked.

"Well, he runs a close second to Jenna, so yeah, he's a good-looking kid."

A nurse took the baby, carried him to a table and began to clean him up. "He's seven pounds and ten ounces and twenty-one inches long," she announced.

Mia gave him a tired smile. "Jarrett, thank you."

He leaned closer to her. "Hey, you did all the work," he said, brushing back her damp hair. He suddenly felt the urge to kiss her. To signify this special moment.

"Yeah, I did, didn't I?" She looked sleepy. "I hate to ask, but would you call Nola? Let her know that I'm okay?"

Jarrett expected she wanted some privacy. He nodded and left. Outside the room he saw Kira hurrying toward him.

"Sorry I'm late." She studied his face and smiled. "I take it the baby's arrived."

He could only nod, feeling his emotions rushing to the surface. "Yeah, it's a boy. Mia and the baby are fine."

She nodded. "And it looks like you did a good job as a stand-in."

He didn't even bother to deny it. "I couldn't leave her."

Kira took his hand. "Be careful, Jarrett. People might mistake you for a good guy," she teased.

"I don't think I have to worry about that." He turned away, wondering when he could see the baby again. "Mia will probably want to see you." He stripped off his cap. "I need a cup of coffee." He started to walk away, but stopped. "Tell Mia I'll be back in a little while."

His sister-in-law studied him for a long time, then said, "Don't look now, brother-in-law, your feelings are showing. It's about time."

Thirty-six hours later, Mia was nearly ready for the trip back home. She and her baby had been checked out, deemed healthy and could be discharged from the hospital.

There was one thing left. She had to put a name on her son's birth certificate. During the night, she'd taken out the letter her brother and sister-in-law had left for her, not to be read until after the birth of their baby.

Mia sat up late to read it and let the tears fall—for the parents who would never know their son, and for the baby who wouldn't have the chance to know them, either.

She opened the envelope.

Dear Mia,

Words can never express the joy and love we feel for you at this moment—the moment we learned that you were pregnant.

Joy and love not only for your unselfish act, not only for giving up a year of your life, but for carrying our child. For that Karen and I will be eternally grateful.

We don't care if this baby is a boy or a girl. But like all mothers, Karen has chosen names for the child. Bradley Preston for a boy or Sarah Margaret for a girl.

Our son or daughter will know what a special person you are. To make sure of that, you will always be a big part of his or her life. Karen and I would like you to be the godmother to little Brad Jr. or Sarah.

If, God forbid, anything should ever happen to either of us, we want you to be the child's guardian. After all, you carried this little miracle in your womb and in your heart for nine months. So who better? Our only other wish is that you find the happiness you truly deserve.

Love always, Brad and Karen.

Mia had sobbed most of the night after that, then the baby was brought to her to be fed. The second she held him in her arms, she knew that she loved him. Yes, BJ was her heart. And he was her son now.

Two hours later, Jarrett parked outside the apartment building and Mia glanced back at the baby.

She still had trouble thinking of herself as a mother.

It didn't take long for a welcoming party to open the door and wave. "Looks like everyone is anxious to see the new resident," Jarrett announced.

That made Mia smile. "BJ's going to have many surrogate grandparents, that's for sure."

"Let's get him inside before they start the inspection," Jarrett said.

He climbed out and came around to the passenger side. He opened the back door and unfastened the baby carrier from its base. "Come on, fella. You've got people to meet."

He raised the carrier's hood and used a blanket to protect the baby from the cold, then lifted him out of the car.

Mia was waiting and took his offered arm as they made their way up the shoveled walk to the door and went in.

"Welcome home, Mia," Nola called along with several other tenants as they walked inside.

"Thank you. It's good to be back."

She glanced around the large entry to see it had been decorated for the holidays. A large tree sat in the center of the area and lights and garlands had been strung along the wrought-iron stairway.

She went to one of the grouping of sofas and

Jarrett placed the baby down on one of the now slip-covered sofas. Mia pulled back the blanket and everyone gasped.

"Oh, he's perfect," Nola cooed and glanced at Mia. "And so handsome, like your brother. What's his name?"

Mia swallowed. "Bradley Preston Saunders, Junior. That's the name Brad and Karen chose. I'm going to call him BJ."

Nola smiled. "It's perfect."

She felt Jarrett's presence behind her. It seemed so natural for him to be there. Too natural.

"I think these two need some rest," Jarrett told everyone.

Normally, Mia wouldn't like him making decisions for her, but she was tired. "Maybe you can come up later."

"Of course, but you need to rest now," Nola added. "If you need someone to watch this little guy, I'm available."

Jarrett picked up the carrier and placed a hand on her elbow as they made their way to the elevator. She was glad she didn't have to climb the stairs. They stepped into the small paneled compartment. He punched the second floor button and the doors closed.

"This is nice," she said.

He frowned. "What, the elevator?"

She nodded. "You have to remember it's been a while since we've been able to ride upstairs."

The doors opened and Jarrett motioned for her to step out first. "Well, only one's working," he said. "The other has multiple problems. I'm going to have to mortgage my home just to fix it."

"You're kidding?"

He suddenly grinned and her heart tripped.

"Almost. These old parts aren't easy to find. But all I need to do is make sure it runs for the next few months."

They reached her apartment and she unlocked the door. Once inside, she tried to take the baby, but Jarrett had already walked into the other room. Her bedroom.

She went after him, knowing it would be best to end this...dependency. She had to do this on her own. No distractions. And Jarrett McKane was definitely a distraction.

"I can handle it from here." Besides she wanted time with her son. Alone.

He set the carrier on the bed and stepped away. "I just didn't want you to lift anything yet." He shrugged. "You just got out of the hospital."

"The baby isn't heavy. Besides, I need to get used to carrying him." She worked to unfasten the straps and he began to stir, then made a little whimpering sound. She lifted him into her arms, feeling the tiny body root against her shoulder. If Jarrett would just leave.

Even though they had shared the birth, she had to draw a line at having an audience while breast-feeding.

"Not a problem."

"I'm sure you have plenty to do. And I need to feed him."

He looked embarrassed as he quickly glanced at his watch. "Sure, I have a meeting anyway." He started out and stopped. "If you need anything…"

"I know, you're across the hall," she echoed, knowing how easy it would be to depend on him. To care more and more for this man. But she had to stand on her own and raise her son. "Jarrett, I could never begin to thank you for everything you've done."

"Hey, what good are landlords if they can't step in as labor coaches?" He glanced at the baby. "Be good to your mom, hot rod." He turned and walked out.

Mia heard the door shut and it sounded so final. But it had to be. She couldn't get involved with Jarrett McKane.

She laid BJ down on the changing table. Startled, the baby blinked open his eyes and looked at her. Something stirred in her chest as his rich blue gaze stared back at her.

"Hey, little guy," she whispered, almost afraid he would start crying. Instead, he stilled at the sound of her voice. Her throat tightened. "Welcome home, son." She swallowed, knowing there could be only one man in her life.

"Looks like it's just you and me now."

CHAPTER EIGHT

A FEW nights later, Jarrett got off the elevator on the second floor after a friendly poker game with Joe and friends in the community room.

Friendly, hah. They were card sharks. All of 'em. They had set him up, and by the time Jarrett had figured it out, it had cost him nearly a hundred bucks. Nothing to do but cut his losses and go home.

Fighting a smile at how the old guys had tricked him, he unlocked his apartment door. Before he got inside he paused, hearing a sound coming from across the hall. A baby crying. BJ. He checked his watch. It was after midnight. He waited a few minutes, but the crying didn't stop. Concerned, he went to Mia's door, and the sound got louder and angrier.

"Mia." He knocked, and after a few seconds the door opened.

A tired and anxious-looking Mia stood on the other side. Dressed for bed, she had on a robe, but by the looks of her, she hadn't gotten much sleep.

"Is everything okay?"

She didn't answer, instead she handed him the baby wrapped in a blanket. "Here, you make him stop. I've tried everything."

He quickly grabbed the bundle, then she turned and walked across the living room.

Jarrett looked down at the red-faced infant with his tiny fists clenched, waving in the air. "Whoa, there, little guy." He closed the door and followed after the mother. "It can't be that bad."

The answer was another loud wail. Not good.

He looked at Mia. "Did you feed him?"

She sent him a threatening look. "Of course I fed him. And I diapered him, bathed him, burped him, but he won't stop crying." Tears filled her eyes, her lower lip trembled. "I'm lousy at this."

"Stop it. You're just new at it."

He readjusted the squirming baby in his arms. Hell, he didn't know what he was doing either. He raised the baby to his shoulder and began rubbing his back. The baby stiffened, but Jarrett didn't stop.

"Has he been eating good?"

Mia nodded, but looked concerned. "Maybe

he's not getting enough. I feed him every two hours."

"Maybe he's got an air bubble," Jarrett said.

He went to the sofa and sat down, laying the screaming baby across his legs. He remembered seeing Kira doing this with Jenna. After a few minutes a burp came from the little guy and the loud crying turned to a few whimpers and then, finally, silence. He kept patting the baby's back until he fell asleep.

He smiled at Mia who still looked close to tears. "Hey, BJ is fine now."

She didn't look convinced.

He lifted the baby into his arms and caught the clean sent of soap as the tiny bundle move against his shoulder, then finally settled down again. Protectiveness stirred in him as he carried the infant into the bedroom.

There was a night-light on over the crib, and he placed BJ down on his back. He made room as Mia adjusted the baby's position and covered him with a blanket. The kid stirred but didn't make another sound. The silence was golden.

They stepped away from the baby's bed. "He's so exhausted, he should sleep for a while," Jarrett said encouragingly.

"Thanks to you," Mia said, then added, "I couldn't even figure out it was gas."

Jarrett took her by the arm and led her across to the queen-size bed. They sat down side by side.

"So now you'll know," he said, seeing the dark circles around her pretty blue eyes. He brushed back wayward strands of hair that had escaped her ponytail. His heart pounded at the surge of desire that shot through him. He needed to leave, but he already knew nothing could draw him away from her.

"Call Kira. She had trouble with Jenna, too. That's how I knew what to do. And the next time you'll know, too."

She swiped at the last of her tears. "You're lucky to have family."

He glanced away. "Trace and Kira didn't always think so." He'd made so many mistakes with his brother.

"You and your brother haven't always been close?" she asked.

"Try never," he admitted. "It was mostly my fault."

"You two look pretty close now."

"Sometimes damage can't be fixed. But thanks to Kira, we've been working on it."

She watched him, waiting for more. "You're half brothers?"

He nodded. "Different mothers. I lost mine

at six." He shrugged. "My dad remarried, and his wife had a baby, Trace."

"Was she a good stepmother?"

"Alice? She didn't have much time for me, so I don't know much about her mothering skills. My dad just dealt with the ranch business, and that included taking me along." He glanced away. "I hated it. I can still smell the stink of the cattle, the burning hide of the steers during branding. And it's damn hard work, for damn little money. And as soon as I could, I got out. Straight into college."

She smiled. "Bet they were proud of you."

"Yeah, sure.

"Brad was my cheering squad. My best friend. Whether I wanted him to be or not." She glanced away. "All I gave him was trouble."

"I can't believe that. I bet you were a good kid."

She shook her head. "I was resentful, head-strong, but mostly stupid. An overweight girl who did anything to fit in. I turned out to be a big disappointment to a lot of people." She released a breath. "So I ran with a crowd that accepted me."

Jarrett could only nod, but he wanted to know so much more about Mia. What had hurt her so much she couldn't talk about it?

"Sometimes we can't see what's right in front

of us." He began. "I took out resentment for my father on Trace. And it was well over thirty years before I figured out he wasn't my enemy. We're still working on it."

She brightened. "I bet little Jenna helps."

He tried not to smile but failed. "Okay, the little squirt has my number. But look at her. She's too cute to tell her no." *So are you,* he nearly confessed, trying to fight the attraction he felt.

"I agree. You are so lucky to have them."

"I'm realizing that." He eyed her closely. "When was the last time you slept?"

She shrugged. "I nap when BJ does."

He breathed a curse. "It's not enough, Mia. You haven't even been out of the hospital a week." Had it been that long since he'd seen her? Since he'd been purposely avoiding her? He'd worked late at the office, staying away to finish the repairs. Anything not to get any more entangled in her life. Trace was the family guy, not him.

Tonight, he realized how much he'd missed her. His gaze went from those brilliant blue eyes to her full mouth. God, he had to be crazy, but he couldn't stop himself as his head lowered to hers.

"Jarrett…"

"I like the way you say my name, Mia. A lot."

He reached for her, pulling her to him until his mouth closed over hers. She released a sigh as her fingers gripped his arms and she leaned into him.

Only the sound of their breathing filled the room as his mouth moved over hers in a slow, sensual, drugging kiss, taking as much as she was willing to give. And he wanted it all.

Hungry. He was hungry for her. His tongue slid past her parted lips and tasted her, but it wasn't enough. He never could get enough of her.

He broke off the kiss and they both drew in needed air. He knew he had to stop, it was too soon for her.

Yet, it was already too late for him.

Mia stirred in the warm bed. It felt so good as she pressed deeper into her pillow. Sleep. She loved just lying in bed. Soon her thoughts turned to last night and Jarrett. The kiss. Smiling, she opened her eyes to the morning light coming through the window, then reality hit her, as she registered her tender breasts.

"BJ," she whispered, throwing back the covers to get out of bed. The crib was empty. Her heart pounded in her chest and she raced out to the other room. That was when she heard a familiar voice in the kitchen. Nola.

She stood in the doorway. "You are getting to be such a big boy," the older woman cooed at the baby in the plastic tub. BJ's tiny arms waved in the air as he enjoyed his bath.

Nola glanced at her. "Well, good morning."

"Good morning, Nola." She brushed her hair back. "What are you doing here? And why didn't you wake me to feed him?"

"He slept most of the night until five o'clock, which is when Jarrett called me and asked about using the bottle of breast milk in the refrigerator. I instructed him on how to heat it and he fed BJ. That was an hour ago, when I came up to relieve him. So I decided to steal some time with this guy while you got some more sleep." She grinned down at the baby, who was cooing. "BJ and I are getting to know each other."

Mia glanced around the empty apartment. When she'd dozed off last night Jarrett was still here. She suddenly recalled several things from their evening together. The things she'd told him about herself. Things she hadn't told anyone.

"If you're looking for Jarrett, he had a meeting to go to. He said he'd be back later today. I hope in time for our Christmas party."

"Who said I was looking for Jarrett?" She hated that she was so easy to read. "Why did he call you instead of waking me?"

"Because we're both worried about you." She

nodded for Mia to hand her the towel. She lifted the baby out of the water and Mia wrapped her son in the hooded terry cloth. "New mothers can get burnt out."

Mia hugged BJ to her. "I need to be able to take care of my son."

"You are a good mother, Mia," Nola assured her. "You're also doing this alone. But you have what's most important, a good heart and a lot of love for this little boy."

Together they walked into the bedroom and dressed BJ in one of his new outfits with a shirt that said, Chick Magnet.

Before Mia could pick him up, Nola did. "You need to eat something first. And I figure you have just enough time for some breakfast and a shower before this guy wants his mommy's attention."

She smiled. How lucky she was to have friends. "Thanks, Nola. I don't know what I'd do without you."

"We owe you a lot, too. We'd all be homeless without your help."

"We'll all be homeless soon anyway. So I didn't help that much."

The older woman pushed her bifocals back in place. "It's not over yet. I have faith in our handsome landlord. I also see the way he looks at you,

Mia." She smiled. "And you should have seen him with BJ this morning. He's a natural."

Mia tried not to think about Jarrett McKane. He wasn't the man for her. He was the kind who only thought about the financial bottom line. Business before family. It was all about profit. The money. "He's counting the days until we're all out of here."

Nola watched her. "Yeah, that's the reason he had us all out to his house for Thanksgiving. And helped Joe paint your apartment. And stayed with you at the hospital during the birth of this little one." She glanced down at the baby, but quickly looked back at Mia. "Jarrett has a few rough edges, but that just makes him interesting." She lowered her voice. "And sexy."

Mia felt heat rise to her face. He had always been the one who'd showed up to help her. She recalled the way he made her feel when he kissed her last night. She hadn't wanted him to stop. That was a problem. If she got involved in a relationship with a man, she had to think about BJ, too. They were a package deal.

Worse yet, could she share all her secrets about her past? Even the lies she'd told to protect herself. What happened when Jarrett discovered who she really was?

* * *

Just a little before noon, Jarrett walked into the restaurant for his meeting. He hoped his lack of sleep last night wouldn't hinder him from convincing Fulton of his new plans. If he kept thinking about Mia and their kiss, it would. Or the fact that he'd left a beautiful woman's bed and gone into the other room to sleep on the sofa. That had been a first for him. There had been a lot of firsts with Mia, including being a babysitter for her son.

When Nola had relieved him from his duties early this morning, he'd had time to shower at his apartment and then go to the office where he'd finished up the presentation for today.

Over the past week or so, he'd been working on new plans for the Fulton factory. He hoped he'd come up with some changes to the construction that would be beneficial to everyone.

And save this deal for him.

If this new idea didn't go over with the CEO, he could lose a lot more than just a sale. Business ventures like this just didn't come down the road every day. It could take years for him to unload this property.

He walked across the restaurant behind the hostess to find Neil at the table by the window. The man didn't look happy, but Jarrett was hopeful he could convince him to make a few concessions.

"Neil, glad you could make it on such short notice."

They shook hands then sat down. "I hope you have some good news. I'd like to finalize this before I fly out tonight."

Jarrett released a quiet breath to calm his nervousness. *Don't let them see you sweat,* his college football coach had always told him. "Then let's get to it," he suggested.

The waitress came by and took their order.

"Now, tell me what's so important." Neil checked his watch. "I have to get on a plane and be back in Chicago tonight for a Christmas party. Robin will kill me if I'm late, especially since we're hosting it."

"It's what I want to show you." Jarrett pulled out the sketches for the plant site. "As you know, I have two apartment buildings located on the property." He took a breath and rushed on. "Because of airtight lease agreements, the remaining tenants aren't moving out until March."

Fulton frowned. "I thought you said you had it handled, that the building would be demolished by the end of January so we could break ground by early spring." Fulton was visibly irritated. "You assured me there wouldn't be a problem."

"Well, a judge stepped in and said otherwise."

Jarrett raised a hand. "So I have another idea that might work even better."

Jarrett opened the folder and presented a sketch of the factory structure. "There's enough land to move the location of the new factory to the back of the property, and put the parking lot in front, leaving the existing apartment buildings."

"And why would I want to do that?" Fulton asked.

"Well, there's a couple of reasons," Jarrett began. "For one thing, it's a better location, a little further from town. So it won't be a traffic nightmare at rush hour."

"It would also cost more for extra materials for laying the utilities," Neil argued.

Jarrett pushed on, hoping his idea would work. "But if you use one of the existing apartment buildings for your corporate offices, you'll save on construction costs."

Neil's brow wrinkled in thought. "You can't be suggesting I use those dilapidated buildings?"

"Use *one* of the buildings," Jarrett corrected. "Why not? They're solidly built. They might have been neglected, but a remodel is a hell of a lot more cost-efficient than brand-new construction, even if you gut it entirely. You'd be recycling and it's better for the environment. And best of all, the building is already vacant. You could start the inside remodel after the holidays. No delay waiting for the ground to thaw."

Jarrett pulled out another drawing. "I had a structural engineer check out the building. It has the fifties retro look, but that can be changed, too. The main thing is it's large enough to house the plant's executive offices. Overall, you'll save money on this project. The shareholders will have to be happy about that."

Fulton didn't say anything for a while as he went over the new plans, then he looked at Jarrett. "There's no way you can remove the tenants?"

Jarrett shook his head. "I can't and won't. The majority are seniors on fixed income and two are disabled. I promised them they could stay until the spring." Then he said something that he never thought he would. "If possible, I'd like them to stay in their apartments for good."

Fulton leaned back in his chair. "You know that there are other locations the board of directors are looking at for this project, don't you?"

Jarrett's gut tightened as he nodded, seeing everything he'd worked for going down the drain. "Yes, I do. But you know this is the best location."

Fulton arched an eyebrow. "These people mean this much to you?"

Jarrett sat back. He hadn't thought about it

until now, but these people been more accepting of him than his own father had. Truth was, they were starting to matter to him. Too much. He thought of Mia and BJ.

He eyed Neil Fulton's expectant look and shrugged. "Hey, I'm just trying to stay out of jail."

Later that evening, when Jarrett returned to the apartment building, he was exhausted. Fulton wouldn't give him an answer, but he had promised to talk it over with the board. Jarrett couldn't ask for any more.

He walked up the sidewalk toward the double doors. If Fulton went along with the new plan it meant Jarrett would keep the apartment building open. Of course, he'd have to put more money into the place, starting with paint. A lot of paint.

He shook his head. It was too soon to get excited. In these economic times nothing was a sure thing.

So Jarrett was in limbo. He thought about last night. Mia Saunders had stormed into his life and begun messing up his perfect plans. He'd liked things his way. Most of his life he'd been able to get what he wanted, until everything started to change, thanks to a blue-eyed do-gooder and her merry band of followers.

Hell, he'd never been a follower, and now look at him. Even worse, he was anxious to see her.

He pulled open the entry door and walked in, surprised to hear the sound of singing. A group of about two dozen tenants stood around an upright piano singing Christmas carols.

Standing back, he watched the people he'd come to know over the past few weeks sharing the joy of the holiday. This was hard for him. He couldn't remember when Christmas had been a happy time. Not since he was a small boy.

Then he spotted Mia across the room and felt a familiar stirring in his gut. She looked pretty, dressed in a blue sweater and her usual black stretch pants. Her dark hair was pulled back and adorned with a red ribbon. Smiling, she waved at him.

Maybe it would be a happy holiday after all.

CHAPTER NINE

MIA caught sight of Jarrett when he walked into the open lobby. It was hard not to notice the man. In a charcoal business suit with a crisp white shirt and a striped tie, covered by a dark trench coat, he looked more Wall Street than small-town Colorado.

"That's one good-looking man."

Mia glanced at Nola who was holding BJ. "Both the McKane men are handsome."

Her friend smiled. "But you're only interested in the older brother." She nudged Mia. "Now, go talk to him before someone else lays claim to your man."

She glared. "He's not mine."

"And he won't be if you keep ignoring him."

Nola gave her another gentle push, sending her off in Jarrett's direction.

Mia hadn't seen much of him, so there hadn't been a chance to invite him to the impromptu party. She couldn't blame him for keeping his distance. He was probably tired of taking care of her.

Besides, why would a man like Jarrett McKane be interested in her? Why would he want to take on a woman with a baby? Yet he'd done so many things for her. He'd been there when she'd needed him the most. How could she not care about a man like that?

Mia discreetly moved around the back of the crowd as Nola watched over BJ. Heart pounding in her ears, she walked up behind him. "You're expected to sing along," she managed to say.

Jarrett turned around to face her. Immediately, she caught the sadness in his eyes before he could mask it. "Everyone will be sorry if I do. My voice is so bad I don't even sing in the shower."

"I can't imagine you doing anything badly." Great. She was acting like an infatuated teenager, and she had never been any good at flirting.

"You'd be surprised at all the things I've messed up." His dark gaze held hers. "Did you get enough sleep last night?"

"Yes, thanks to you," she said, wondering if he'd thought about their kiss. Her gaze went to his mouth, then she quickly glanced away. "And thank you for not bringing up my meltdown."

Jarrett couldn't stop looking at Mia. Blue was

definitely her color, bringing out the richness of her eyes.

"What meltdown?" he said, trying hard to focus on what she was saying. "You were just exhausted from lack of sleep and worried about your baby."

He couldn't help but remember how, during the night, he'd kept going in to watch her sleep. How strange was that? "I hope you got enough rest."

She nodded. "Plenty. And you're a good neighbor for coming to my rescue."

He tensed. Neighbor? *What neighbor kisses you like I did?* "That's me, just the full-service landlord," he said, trying to keep the sarcasm out of his voice. He started to leave, but she put her hand on his arm.

"Jarrett, what I meant was you went beyond helping me." Her eyes searched his face. "I've asked far too much of you. BJ and I weren't part of the deal when you were ordered to move in here."

"Did you hear me complain?"

She shook her head. "You should. I feel like I've taken advantage."

"Like I said, I haven't minded."

"And I'm grateful for everything—"

Grasping her hand on his arm, Jarrett leaned forward. The memory of last night's kiss had him aching for another. "I didn't do it for your gratitude, Mia."

He watched her swallow quickly, but before she could speak, the singing stopped and someone called to him.

"Unca Jay! Unca Jay!" Jenna came running toward him. "You're here."

He swung the child up in his arms. She had on a pretty sweater with snowflakes and dark pants.

"I have to go to work," he told her. "What are you doing here?"

"It's a Christmas party, silly. We got invited to come and sing." Her big blue eyes rounded. "You know what else?"

He played along. "No, what else?"

"It's only two more days 'til Christmas, and Mommy and Daddy asked everybody to come to our house for Christmas dinner. Even Mia and her new baby, BJ. And I got to hold him."

Jarrett looked across the room and saw his brother and Kira walking toward them. "How nice."

He got a hug from Kira and a handshake from Trace. "So, the festivities are at your house?"

Trace nodded. "Same as every year, but with Jody and Nathan gone, Kira's a little lonely. So why not have a big crowd?"

Jarrett looked at his sister-in-law.

"I love to cook," Kira said. "Besides, Nola and the others are bringing food, too. It's not much different than the group we had at your house on Thanksgiving."

"And now we have baby BJ," Jenna added as she patted her own chest and looked at Jarrett. "Unca Jay, did you know that BJ drinks milk from Mia's breasts?"

"Jenna…" her mother said with a warning look.

Everyone bit back a chuckle while Jarrett exchanged a look with Mia that felt far too intimate. Oh, yeah, he knew that.

His niece drew his attention back to her. "Look, Unca Jay." She pointed up to the sprig of greenery hanging overhead in the doorway. "Mistletoe."

Great. "It sure is." He leaned forward and placed a noisy kiss on the girl's cheek.

That wasn't the end of it; Jenna wiggled to be put down. "Now, you gotta kiss Mia."

Jarrett looked at a blushing Mia. "Sure." He leaned forward and placed a chaste kiss on her cheek. Their eyes met as he pulled back.

"No, not like that," Jenna insisted. "Like Mommy and Daddy do it. Put your arms around her and you have to touch lips for a long time."

Jarrett eyed his brother as Trace shrugged,

trying not to smile. He got no help as he turned back to Mia. Without giving her a chance to protest, he reached for her and pulled her into his arms. His gaze locked onto her mesmerizing eyes, and, once his mouth closed over hers, everything and everyone else in the room faded away. It was all Mia and how she made him feel. How she tasted, how her scent drifted around him, how he was barely keeping himself in control.

Finally cheers broke out, and he tore his mouth away. "Did I do it okay?" he asked his niece.

A smiling Jenna nodded her head. He turned back to the woman in his arms. "Suddenly, I'm getting into the Christmas spirit."

Mia glanced at her kitchen clock and debated whether to attend the services tonight. For the first time in ten years, it wouldn't be Reverend Bradley Saunders standing at the pulpit delivering her Christmas Eve sermon. The last three years he'd been the pastor here in Winchester Ridge.

Mia had only been nineteen when Bradley had rescued her from self-destruction and got her on the road to recovery. From then on she'd sat in the front pew, grateful she had the love of family, and a future.

She glanced down at her son in the carrier. BJ would have the same; she would make sure of that.

"It's just us now, kid." She smiled as BJ, dressed in his dark-green holiday outfit, reacted to her voice with a cooing sound. "I might be new at this mother stuff, but no one could love you more." She wished she could give him a traditional family. Every kid deserved a mother and a father.

"I guess we'd better get going, or we'll be late."

She checked her own Christmas outfit, her standard black stretch pants and a long red sweater she'd found in a drawer.

After putting on her coat and BJ's cap and tucking a blanket around him, she picked up the carrier and walked out. She glanced across the hall to Jarrett's apartment.

As much as she tried not to, she'd thought about Jarrett a lot over the last few days. Okay, so it had been from the day he'd moved in. Not that she'd wanted him in her life; he'd just sort of barged into it.

At first, she'd even tried to compare Jarrett to her father, but she quickly realized they were nothing alike. Preston Saunders would never open his home to a bunch of strangers for Thanksgiving dinner. Nor would he give up his time to help paint a room for her baby son, or even stay and play coach as she gave birth.

Mia touched her lips thinking about the shared kisses. Even though Jarrett had been goaded into the one under the mistletoe, he hadn't acted as if he minded at all. Yet he hadn't exactly shown up at her door the past thirty-six hours wanting to continue what had been started either.

Suddenly the elevator doors opened and Jarrett got off. He immediately smiled. "Hello, Mia."

"Jarrett," she said, trying to act casual. He looked too good in his jeans and sweater with a sheepskin jacket hanging open and his cowboy hat cocked just a little. "Merry Christmas."

He raised his arm to check his watch and she noticed the big shopping bags. "Is it that time already?" He eyed her closely. "I guess I'd better finish up my wrapping." He glanced at BJ. "Where are you two headed?"

"To the Christmas service at the church."

His smile faded. "Give me a second and I'll drive you."

"Jarrett, no. I can't let you do that. I can drive myself. We're not going that far."

"There's a lot of snow still on the roads, and your tires aren't in that great a shape."

He was right, but she hadn't had a chance to replace them. "It's only a few miles."

"And you have precious cargo." He nodded at

her son and pulled out his keys. "Then at least take my SUV. It's four-wheel drive."

He was letting her drive his car? She looked at him, telling herself not to read anything into it. It was for her ten-day-old son. She decided to test him.

"Okay, I'll let you drive us, but only if you stay for the service."

He frowned. "You're kidding, right?"

She shook her head.

"It's been a long time since I've been inside a church."

"It's not going to crumble down around you. C'mon, you can handle it. You're a big strong guy," she challenged him.

He hesitated and finally relented. "Okay, just let me drop these presents off in the apartment."

She hadn't really thought he'd come, but suddenly she was glad she didn't have to face this night alone. Nor did she mind spending Christmas Eve with this man.

Nearly two hours later, Jarrett stood in the back of the church, watching as the parishioners fussed over BJ. Mia was enjoying showing off her son. She'd put up a brave front, but he knew it had been hard for her to come back here without her brother, her family.

He glanced around the ornate stone building with the stained-glass windows and high ceilings. He remembered another church across town where his stepmother had insisted they go to services weekly. And the Sunday school teacher who swore that a young Jarrett's bad attitude would send him straight to hell.

That hadn't been a good time in Jarrett's life. His mother had died suddenly when he was barely six, and within a few months his father had another wife. The following year his baby brother, Trace, had been born. And the struggle between the McKane brothers had begun. The father he'd so badly needed after the loss of his mother, turned away and found another family. Jarrett had been told he had to carry more weight and help out. Suddenly there wasn't any time to be a kid, or time to be with the father he'd needed so desperately.

He quickly pushed aside the bad memories. Tomorrow was Christmas, and, thanks to Kira, he and Trace were finally working on liking each other.

Family wasn't the only thing that gave him trouble; he was still hoping to hear from Fulton.

He'd closed the office early today, but Neil had his cell phone number. If the land deal crashed, *no one* would have a happy holiday. He might even end up being a permanent resident in the Mountain View Apartments.

He glanced across at Mia. Not that he would mind being her neighbor. If he was honest, he was happy that he got to spend time with her tonight. He tried to tell himself it was only because he felt protective of the new mother. But he was attracted to her, big-time. As much as he'd tried to stay away, she kept drawing him back into her life. He sure as hell wasn't putting up much resistance, either.

Mia walked over to him. "I'm sorry I kept you waiting. Everyone wanted to see BJ."

"Well he's a cute kid, and you should be a proud mama. It's okay if you want to stay."

She shook her head as she pulled the carrier hood up and covered the baby. "I really need to feed BJ. Could we go home?"

"Sounds good." He took the carrier from her and escorted her through the doors. Once outside they were greeted by a strong wind and snow flurries. He pulled Mia close against his side, trying to shield her from the biting cold.

At the SUV, he helped Mia get in and quickly latched BJ's safety seat in the back, then he climbed in the driver's seat and started the engine.

Glancing out the window, he waited for the cab to warm up. "I was afraid of this."

She was shivering. "I'm sorry. I didn't think the weather would turn bad. It's supposed to be clear tomorrow."

Her coat wasn't heavy enough to keep her warm. He flipped the heater on high and took a blanket from the back seat to drape over her legs. "We're lucky it's not a big storm, just the tail end of it. But I'll feel better when we're back at the apartment."

Jarrett pulled out of the parking lot cautiously. He glanced at the baby in the back seat; he was starting to fuss.

"Hang on, BJ. We'll be home soon."

Jarrett turned off the main street onto a back road, thinking he could shave off some time. First mistake—the road was deserted. Secondly, it hadn't been cleared of snow. Even with four-wheel drive, traction was nonexistent.

"Sorry, this was a bad idea. I'll turn back."

BJ began to cry louder.

Jarrett found a wide spot in the road and slowed more as he began to turn the wheel. He cursed when the back of the vehicle began to slide. "Hang on," he called to Mia. He gripped the wheel tighter, turning into the slide, but he couldn't gain control. When he got the car stopped they were off the side of the road.

Jarrett cursed under his breath and BJ let out a wail. Shifting into Reverse, he backed up, but nothing happened. He tried going forward again, but the only thing he got was the spinning of the tires as the car slipped sideways, deeper into the snowbank. Although angry with himself, he remained calm. "I'll go see if I can dig us out."

"Be careful," Mia called over the screams of the baby.

Placing his hat on his head, Jarrett got out and made it through the ankle-high snow to the back of the car. He opened the hatch and took out a shovel. He began digging, but soon discovered it was useless. He made his way back to the driver's side and climbed in. Pulling off his gloves, he took out his phone. "We need a tow truck." He punched in his roadside assistance. By the time he hung up, he wasn't happy. "She put us at the top of the list because of the baby, but it still could be an hour."

"Long as we're warm, it's okay," she said. "Do you have enough gas?"

"Yeah, a full tank."

"Good. I need to feed BJ. I'll go in the back."

"No, stay up here, it's warmer." He flipped on the interior light, leaned into the back seat and managed to unfasten the crying baby's straps.

"Come on, little guy, settle down," he coaxed. "You'll have your mama in a minute." He lifted the small bundle and handed him to Mia who had already removed her coat, leaving it draped over her shoulders.

She looked at him and paused. "Would you mind turning off the light?"

"Oh, sure." Of course she didn't want an audience.

In the dark, he could see her tug up her sweater. All at once there was silence. Jarrett looked over at Mia as she leaned over the child at her breast, stroking him.

His chest tightened at the scene. Finally turning away, he concentrated on the snow blowing across the front window, but he could still hear Mia's soft voice as she talked to her son. Leaning back against the headrest, he closed his eyes and tried not to think about how much he wanted to wrap his arms around both of them and protect them. Yeah, he'd done a great job of that so far.

Restless, he sat up. "Life is pretty simple to him, food and Mama." He looked at her as she moved the baby to her shoulder and began to pat his back.

"Sometimes it scares me that I have someone who's so dependent on me," she admitted.

"You're a natural at this."

She paused. "How can you say that when you've seen me at my worst?"

BJ gave a burp and she lowered him to her other breast. This time Jarrett didn't turn away from the silhouette of mother and son. He'd never seen anything so beautiful. Leaning across the console, he reached out and touched the baby's head. "I've only seen a mother who loves her child." His chest tightened at the sight.

Their gazes met in the dark car. "I do love him. At first I was so frightened, but he's become my life. I know technically he's my nephew, but—"

Jarrett placed his finger against her mouth to stop her words. "In every way that counts, Mia, he's your son. You carried him in your womb, now you nourish him from your body." His fingers moved and grazed her breasts. "It's beautiful to watch you with him."

"Oh, Jarrett."

At the husky sound of her voice, he shifted closer. He felt her breath against his cheek.

Suddenly a bright light shone through the windshield, illuminating the front seat. He drew his hand away, but continued to hold her gaze.

"It seems we've been rescued," he said, knowing he wasn't so sure about his heart.

CHAPTER TEN

It was after eleven o'clock by the time the tow truck pulled Jarrett's SUV out of the snowdrift and they'd driven back to the apartment. The night had been long, but still Mia didn't want their time together to end.

Jarrett walked her to her apartment door. "I'm sorry about tonight. I never should have taken that back road." He glanced at BJ in the carrier. "I would never do anything to endanger either one of you."

"Of course I know that. You didn't cause the bad weather, Jarrett."

He watched her a moment, then he finally said. "I probably should let you get some sleep."

She put her hand on his arm when he started to step back. "Won't you come in for some coffee?" Did she sound desperate? "I have something for you."

He looked surprised. "Okay, but let me grab

something from my place first. I'll be back in a few minutes."

With a nod, Mia went into the apartment, leaving the door unlocked. She quickly dressed her son in his sleeper and put him in the crib, knowing in just a few hours he'd be awake and hungry. She checked her makeup and went back into the living area, quickly picked up several baby items scattered around and tossed them into her bedroom.

She'd finished plugging in the lights on her tabletop Christmas tree when there was a soft knock. She tugged on her sweater and brushed back her hair before answering the door.

"Oh, my," she gasped as Jarrett walked in carrying several presents. "What did you do?"

He set the packages down on the table. "I took Jenna shopping yesterday and she convinced me that BJ had to have all these things." He raised an eyebrow. "You should have seen what I talked her out of."

Mia eyed the boxes, but picked up the stuffed bear. "He isn't even sitting up yet."

"Then put some away for his birthday." He smiled and her heart tripped.

She glanced toward the present under her tree. Before she lost her nerve, she grabbed the tissue-wrapped gift and handed it to him. "This is for you."

He looked touched. "Mia, I didn't expect anything."

She shrugged as if it were nothing. "It's probably silly."

He tore through the paper and uncovered the charcoal-gray scarf she'd knitted. As he examined it she wondered if he could see the mistakes.

He stared at her, his brown eyes tender. "Did you make this?"

She managed a nod. "Nola taught me while I was on bed rest. I'm not very good."

She didn't get to finish as he leaned forward and placed a sweet kiss on her mouth. Chaste or not, she felt dizzy.

"Thank you. I've never received anything so nice."

Jarrett had trouble holding it together. He hadn't enjoyed the holidays for a long time. His mother's death only days before Christmas had left a little boy devastated with grief.

"You're welcome," she said, her voice hoarse.

He finally stepped back and draped the scarf around his neck before he lost all control. "I have something for you."

"Did Jenna pick it out, too?"

"No, I did." He pulled a small jewelry box from the bag. "So I can't blame her if you don't like it."

She blinked seeing the store name on the box. "Oh, Jarrett, you shouldn't have done this."

He smiled at her. "You haven't even seen it. Maybe you won't like it."

She gave him a stern look. "Of course I will." She opened the box to see a sterling-silver chain with a round charm engraved with BJ's name and his date of birth.

She glanced at him. "I was wrong, I don't like it. I love it. Oh, Jarrett. It's perfect. You couldn't have gotten me anything I wanted more."

He released a breath. He'd bought women gifts before. Why did he care so much about this one? "I'm glad."

She took it out of the box. "Will you help me put it on?" She gave him the necklace and turned around. Moving aside her rich brown hair, she exposed her long slender neck to him. Somehow, he managed to fasten the clasp, but she was too tempting not to lean down and place a kiss against her exposed skin.

He felt her shiver, but she didn't move. He slid his hands around her waist, pulling her against him. He whispered her name and after a few seconds, he turned her in his arms. "This isn't a good idea. In fact it's crazy. You just had a baby, and I shouldn't be thinking…"

"Oh, Jarrett." She shook her head. "I don't see how… I'm having enough trouble trying to handle my life. You've seen me at the worst times, and you have to be tired of rescuing me."

"Maybe I like rescuing you." He didn't let her go. He had no business wanting her. He was all wrong for her. But all he wanted was to be with her.

"I want to be self-reliant."

"We all like to be. But there are some things that are fun to do with someone else, someone special."

He dipped his head and captured her mouth. His arms circled her and he pulled her close as he deepened the kiss, tasting the addicting sweetness that was only Mia.

With the last of his control, he broke off the kiss, and pressed his forehead against hers. "You're big trouble, lady."

Before she could say anything, the clock chimed. Midnight.

"Merry Christmas, Mia."

Even though the air was brisk, the day promised to be bright and sunny. A perfect Colorado Christmas, Mia thought as she fingered the charm on her necklace.

She glanced across the SUV at Jarrett. Christmas Eve had already been wonderful and this morning had started out close to perfect, too. Jarrett had showed up with a box of jelly donuts and they'd shared breakfast together. Just the three of them.

It could give a girl ideas. Ideas she had no business thinking when she should only be thinking about her son.

Although the man was definitely making this holiday memorable, especially when he'd insisted on taking her and BJ out to the ranch today. Were they a couple? No. She shook away that crazy thought.

"We're here."

Jarrett's voice drew her attention as he turned off the main highway and drove under an arch announcing the McKane Ranch.

Mia felt the excitement as a large two-story house came into view. She smiled at the snowman in the front yard, then her attention went to the wraparound porch and the dark shutters that framed the numerous windows.

Jarrett bypassed the driveway and went around the house. "We're pretty informal here," he said. "I don't think the front door has been opened in years. Everyone has always used the back door."

That would never be allowed in her parents' home. The service entrance was only for the hired help. "Sounds like my kind of place. I bet you had fun growing up here."

His smiled faded. "Ranching is a lot of work. One of the reasons I left and went away to college."

He parked next to Joe and Sylvia's car at the small porch that overlooked the barn and corral. "So now the place belongs to Trace."

He turned off the engine. "After our parents died, I was happy to sell him my half."

She smiled. "You can still come back whenever you want, and the best part is seeing your family."

There was a long pause, then he said, "There was a long time when I wasn't exactly welcome. But a few years ago, Trace and I became partners in a natural gas lease. The money helps him keep the ranch and not worry about having to run cattle. And I can invest in business ventures. Anyway, then Jenna came along, and somehow I ended up calling by more and we sorted some things out."

Mia was surprised by Jarrett's admission. "Well, I'm glad you and your family have reconciled your differences."

He nodded and turned toward the house. "Oh, look, here comes the welcoming committee."

Kira and Trace stepped onto the porch. "Welcome and Merry Christmas."

Mia got out and the cold breeze brushed

against her cheeks. "Merry Christmas," she called back.

Trace came down the shoveled steps and greeted his brother first, then walked around the car to her. "Welcome, Mia."

"Thank you for inviting us. Your place is beautiful."

"We think so." He glanced at his brother. "There's plenty of time before dinner so you can leave BJ with us while Jarrett shows you around." He pointed toward a group of bare trees. "The cottage is just over there, if you're still interested in seeing it."

Mia turned around to see a small white structure about fifty yards from the house. "Oh, yes. I'd love to."

Jarrett got BJ from the back seat while Mia handed a large poinsettia plant to Trace.

When Jarrett's brother started to protest, citing the no-gift clause, she quickly said, "It's from BJ."

With a smile, she retrieved a salad and a pie and carried them into a huge country kitchen with maple cabinets and granite countertops filled with food. Several mouthwatering aromas surrounded her, making her hungry.

Nola and Sylvia were already there helping Kira with the meal. "Just put those things down, if you can find a spot for them."

Kira beamed as she came up to Jarrett and gave him a kiss on the cheek, and then looked down at the carrier. "I'd love to get my hands on this little guy, if I could."

"Sure," Mia told her. "He loves being held."

It took only seconds before Kira had BJ in her arms. "Now you two run off and see the cottage. We can handle things here."

Jarrett came up beside Mia. "They seem to be trying to get rid of us."

"Not at all, but I would love to have this little guy around more." Kira smiled down at the baby and cooed, "Oh, yes I would."

"Let's go." Jarrett escorted Mia out the door and across the yard, but she was distracted by the horses roaming around in the corral.

"Oh, what beautiful animals."

Jarrett changed direction as they detoured to the corral fence. "Trace has been doing some horse-breeding the past few years. This guy is Thunder Road." When he whistled, the horse trotted over as Jarrett climbed up on the fence railing so he could pet the spirited animal. "Hey, Roady." He rubbed the horse's face and neck briskly, then glanced at Mia. "This guy was sired by Midnight Thunder, a champion cutting horse."

"He's beautiful." She could see how much

Jarrett loved animals. "He seems to like you, too."

"He knows me. I come out here sometimes."

There was so much about this man she didn't know, that he kept hidden. She glanced around. "I still can't see how you'd want to give this place up. I love the peace and quiet."

He shrugged and released the horse and they watched him run off. "When I was younger, I called it boredom. I wanted excitement and fun." He looked toward the horses. "After my mother died, my father and I didn't get along much."

Mia understood that. "He's gone now?"

"Yeah. When his wife died, he wasn't much for living alone."

"What about your mother?"

He continued to stare toward the corral. "She's been gone since I was a kid."

"I'm sorry, Jarrett. How old were you?"

"Six."

"Oh, God, you were just a child."

He turned toward her. She could see the pain before he quickly masked it. "I grew up fast."

"What about your stepmother?" She wanted him to tell her that she'd been a caring and loving woman. "Did she help you through that time?"

"I don't remember much." He shifted. "She was just there, and soon, so was Trace."

"At least you had a brother to share things with."

"Yeah, right. I did everything possible to let him know how much I hated him."

Jarrett stepped up to the small cottage porch and turned to see if Mia needed help. Damn, he hated that he'd spilled his guts to her. He'd never told anyone about his childhood. Why her?

He inserted the key into the lock. "I know Trace and his foreman, Cal, redid the entire inside."

"The outside is well-maintained, too," she said, coming up beside him. "I can't wait to see the rest."

He swung open the front door, and they stepped into a living room that had a small sofa and two chairs. An area rug covered part of the shiny hardwood floors.

"Oh, this is nice."

He gestured with his hand to go on, and she walked into a galley-style kitchen. All the stained-wood cabinets were new, as were the egg-shell-colored solid-surface countertops. The white appliances gleamed. Jarrett had no doubt Kira had been out here cleaning.

"This is so nice. There's even a table and chairs." Mia walked through to a small sunroom that looked toward the open pastures.

"This would be a perfect work area. Plenty of light and space for a desk and computer."

She beamed as she walked ahead of him and down the hall. She stuck her head into the bathroom that also had a stackable washer and dryer. "Okay, I've died and gone to heaven." She went on to check out the two bedrooms. When she came out she looked about to burst.

Her dark hair was bouncing against her shoulders. And he noticed how slim she was becoming, and how long her legs were. Yet, it was her eyes, those blue eyes of hers that made his gut tighten in need.

"This is three times as big as my apartment," she said, bringing him back to the present.

"And thirty miles out of town." But closer to his house. "In the winter that could be a difficult drive."

"But I know I can afford this place," she insisted. "Obviously, if I stay here, I plan to pay rent to Kira and Trace."

He studied the stubborn woman in front of him. She was beautiful and no doubt capable of doing anything she set her mind to.

"Okay, but you have to let me take you to look for a dependable car. That sedan of yours is in bad shape."

Her eyes widened. "I can't afford a new car."

"Not new, but at least an upgrade from what you're driving now. I can get you a good deal, one with decent tires."

She smiled slowly. "You're a fraud, Jarrett McKane. You try to get everyone to think you're this ruthless businessman with no heart, but you're a nice guy."

He stood straighter. "If you think I've gone soft because I'm fixing the apartments up, think again. I have a good reason for doing it. The judge ordered me to."

Her look told him she wasn't buying it.

"Ah, hell. At least while you're living there I can keep an eye on you."

"You're not responsible for me, Jarrett," she told him sternly. "I can take care of myself, and have for a lot of years."

"I know that." He couldn't help wondering about other men in her life. "What if I just want to help you?" He tested her. "Say if I want to come around to see if you and BJ need anything? I mean, I do visit my brother and sister-in-law out here."

"And Jenna," Mia added.

"And Jenna," he repeated, watching the light play off her hair. Her skin looked so soft.

Her eyes met his. "Aren't you going to be too busy with the new factory project to bother with us?"

He shrugged. "That's not a done deal, yet. I'm still going over things with Fulton Industries."

"It's because of the tenants, isn't it?"

"Things could work out better." He didn't want to tell her his idea to keep the apartment building. "Hey, what's the worst that can happen? The deal goes south and I get to live in the hellhole apartment 203 forever."

"Well, BJ and I would be your neighbors."

He stepped closer. "I thought you were moving in here?"

"Not if the apartment is still available. I like paying my own way. Would you raise the rent on us?"

He smiled at her. "Maybe we can work out a special deal."

An hour later, with BJ asleep in his carrier in the living room, the Christmas dinner could start.

In the McKanes' dining room, there were two long tables dressed with red and green tablecloths and holiday china. A row of delicious food dishes crowded the sideboard, not to mention the overflow waiting in the kitchen, along with a dozen pies and assorted desserts.

Mia carried her heaping plate to the table to find a seat. It was no surprise Jarrett had saved one next to him.

"This is the best Christmas ever." Jenna

climbed into a booster seat next to her uncle. "And you know what else, Unca Jay?"

The youngster didn't wait for prompting. "I'm glad you bringed BJ and Mia. And that you aren't mad at Daddy anymore."

Mia caught the exchange between the two brothers who sat across from each other.

"Yeah, well it's Christmas," Jarrett said. "Everyone should get along."

"It's a time for peace and goodwill," Joe added. "And we should think about those who aren't here with us today."

"Like Jody and Nathan," Jenna said. "And Ben, 'cause he's protecting our country."

"That he is," Nola said. "We need to pray for all servicemen who are away from their families, too. And to keep them safe."

Everyone bowed their heads as Trace led them in the blessing. Mia was surprised when Jarrett took her hand in his. It was warm and reassuring. She was glad that she had someone to share this day with.

"Now, let's eat," Jarrett announced after the prayer. And it began. Lively conversation and good food.

"Mia, how did you like the cottage?"

She looked across the table at Kira. "Oh, I love it. It's beautiful and so roomy."

Kira exchanged a look with her husband. "Does that mean you plan to move in?"

"If you still want us, I'd love to move out here."

A big smile spread across Kira's face. "That's wonderful." She looked at her brother-in-law. "And it's not so inconvenient living out here. We have good neighbors. How far away is your place, Jarrett? Five miles?"

Jarrett's fork paused on its way to his mouth. "Something like that."

His sister-in-law was grinning now. "See, there's a McKane around if you need one, and also we have Cal here, too."

The foreman looked up from the other end of the table and nodded. "It would be nice to have another little one around the place."

Trace stood up. "Speaking of little ones." He glanced down at his wife and exchanged a look that showed everyone in the room how much they loved one another. "We have some news, and we thought that this would be a perfect day to share it. Kira and I are expecting our second child next summer."

Jarrett watched as the room erupted in cheers and congratulations. He suddenly felt the old jealousy creeping in. Why would he be jealous of a baby? He'd never wanted a family.

He turned to Mia, who was watching him.

"Isn't that wonderful news?"

"Yeah, it is." He glanced at his brother. "Hey, Trace. Congratulations."

Jenna finally got into the act. "Am I going to have a baby sister? I asked for a sister."

Everyone laughed.

"We don't know if it's a girl or boy, yet," Kira told her daughter. "But I know you'll be happy with either."

Before Jenna could speak, the sound of BJ's crying drew everyone's attention.

"Someone's hungry. Excuse me," Mia said as she left the table.

Jarrett wanted to go with her, but he had no right to share this time with her and her son. He saw Kira direct her upstairs to a bedroom.

Again he was on the outside looking in, where he'd been for so many years. He didn't want to be there anymore.

Mia sat in the rocking chair in the McKane nursery. Once the room had been Jenna's, but the toddler had been moved to another bedroom and a big girl's bed. How convenient that Trace and Kira already had a beautiful room for their next baby.

She smiled down at her son, and her heart nearly burst with love. She could no longer see her life without this child. He was everything to her, and she would do everything she could to give him a good life. She'd find a way to finish law school and make a home for him. She ran her hand over his head. "I promise you this, BJ, I'll be the best mom I can."

Her thoughts turned to Jarrett. Would he be a part of their lives? Would he come around once she moved out here? Once the apartment building was demolished, he'd be so involved in the factory project she doubted there would be time for her.

Mia fingered the chain around her neck. She was a realist, and couldn't lie to herself. Jarrett wasn't the type of man who took on a woman with a baby. Yet, she recalled him telling her about his mother's death, and his stepmother's neglect. She thought back to her own youth. Seemed they weren't so different after all.

BJ stiffened and began to fuss. "I think you need a burp." She brought him to her shoulder and began to pat his back gently. BJ cried louder. "Sshh, honey. Relax." She continued the rubbing, but it wasn't working.

There was a knock on the door and Jarrett peered in. "Sounds like someone isn't happy."

Mia was both confused and relieved as Jarrett walked in. "You want to try?"

He took the infant from her. He placed her son against his large chest and began to walk and pat. After about thirty seconds, the crying stopped when a burp erupted from the infant.

Jarrett smiled at her. "Looks like I still have the touch."

"Then I'll give you BJ's feeding schedule and you can come by and do the honors."

She didn't hide her smile at his surprised look.

"You know I will if you need me," he said sincerely.

"Don't, Jarrett. I can't keep relying on you to help me." Even if she wanted nothing more than to have him around all the time. "BJ is my responsibility."

He came closer, but wouldn't relinquish the baby. "Why, Mia? Why do you think you have to do this all by yourself?"

She glanced away from those velvet-brown eyes. "It's safer that way, Jarrett. And no one gets hurt."

He touched her chin and turned her back to him. "Who hurt you, Mia? What man broke your heart?"

She stiffened and shook her head. "It's not important. It was a long time ago."

"It's important to me. You're important to me, Mia."

She wanted so much to believe him, but she

wasn't good when it came to trust. "Oh, Jarrett. I don't know what to say."

He stepped in closer. "Good. I'd rather do this." Even with BJ against his shoulder, he leaned down to capture her mouth and quickly had her heart racing and her body stirring, wanting more.

He broke off as BJ began to complain. "Maybe we can talk more about this later." He gave her another peck and straightened up just as Kira walked in.

"I hate to disturb you both, but there's someone here to see you, Mia."

"Who?"

"He says he's your father."

CHAPTER ELEVEN

MIA had been dreading this day for ten years. Why did he have to find her? Why now? She saw the confused look on Jarrett's face, not surprising as she'd told everyone she had no family.

As far as she was concerned, since Brad's death, there hadn't been anyone. Putting a sleeping BJ in the crib, she finally looked at Jarrett. "Please, don't say anything about the baby."

He stared at her a moment, but his expression didn't give anything away. "I'll follow your lead."

They walked out and down the stairs, grateful that Kira had put the unexpected guest in the living room, away from everyone. She glanced at Jarrett. "I need to talk to him alone."

He nodded. "I'll be close by."

With a sigh, she walked into the room. Preston Elliot Saunders stood in front of the massive stone fireplace. Since his back was to her, she took the opportunity to study him. Still tall and trim, his once thick dark hair was now nearly white and there was a slight slump to his shoulders. He turned slightly and she could see he wore a dark wool coat over a business suit.

Had she ever seen him when he hadn't been in a suit? As a child she'd only seen him when she needed to be disciplined. She'd been the daughter who couldn't seem do anything right, so that had been a lot.

Preston finally turned around and she saw that the last decade had added lines to his face. She hoped to see some emotion from him, but, once again, she was disappointed.

She fought off all the old fears and insecurities and stepped fully into the room. "You wanted to see me?"

He frowned. "After all this time that's all you have to say to me?"

"Ten years ago I was a disgrace to the family and was destroying my life. You disowned me and sent me away. So excuse my surprise when you show up here now. There must be a reason." She knew exactly the reason. Somehow he'd learned about her baby.

"No matter what happened between us, you should have had the decency and compassion to tell me about Bradley's death. Your mother and I were heartbroken when we learned about it recently."

Mia noted he didn't mention his daughter-in-law's death. Not only had Preston and Abigail disapproved of their son's chosen profession, they had made their disdain at his choice of a wife perfectly clear. Karen hadn't come from the right family. "It's been years since you disowned us, so why would I think you wanted to know about Brad's death?"

Her father looked sad. "For God sake's, Margaret, we're family."

"Since when? We weren't a family. A family man comes home. You were never there, and when you were, all you did was criticize."

Preston straightened. "You know perfectly well why I did what I did. You were out of control. An embarrassment to yourself and everyone else. We tried to warn Bradley."

Mia tried to hide her surprise. Her brother had contacted their father? "Did you expect him to send me away, or have me locked up in a place where I lived like a prisoner?" She shivered in memory. "Like you had?" She spread her arms. "I've gone to college, and I can support myself. Well take a good look, I'm perfectly fine. Have been for years. So now that you've checked on me, you can go home with a clear conscience." She turned to leave, praying this would be the end.

"Not so fast, Margaret. There's some unfinished business to do with my grandson."

Mia swung around as a fierce protectiveness took over. "He's not your grandchild. You didn't want to be a part of my life or Brad's because we refused to do what you wanted. So you have no claim on this baby."

Preston Saunders frowned. "You're wrong, Margaret. My family has always come first, which is why I'm here." He glared at her. "You can't possibly think you can give Bradley's son the life I can. I've seen where you live. You have nothing to offer him. The boy would be much better off with your mother and me."

"That's not true. Besides I can give him love, which is more than you and Mother ever did. Brad and Karen wanted me to raise their child if something happened to them."

Her father's gaze moved over her. "I don't want my grandchild living in that slum apartment."

"Not that it's any of your business, but I'll be moving soon into a two-bedroom house. I have income and I'll be going back to law school. I can support BJ. And that's all that you need to know."

He studied her for a long moment. "I know more than you might think. And I don't want you moving in with this Jarrett McKane."

She was shaking. "My personal life is none of your business."

Her father stood his ground. "You're wrong. I've asked around. Your ex-football player may have had minimal success during his college career, and even in this small town, but things can change quickly."

Mia hated that this man could still get to her. And he was planning to use her friendship with Jarrett. "What is that supposed to mean?"

He shrugged. "These are hard times, and business deals can easily fall apart. Just recently I was discussing this with Neil Fulton. What a coincidence that his wife, Robin, and your mother were sorority sisters." A smug look appeared across his face. "From what Neil tells me, it's still up in the air about where their new factory is going to be built."

Mia felt sick to her stomach. "This has nothing to do with Jarrett. It's between you and me."

"Then all you have to do is give me what I want."

Jarrett stood in the hallway. If Mia had let everyone think that her parents were dead, there had to be a reason, and he couldn't wait to hear it.

"Is there a problem?" Trace asked coming up to him.

"Not sure." Jarrett had no idea what was going

on. "But I plan to find out." When he heard Mia tell her father goodbye, he went into action. He walked into the living room.

"Is everything okay?" He went over to Mia, slipping a possessive arm around her back.

She looked surprised to see him. "Yes. My father was just leaving."

The man didn't move, just turned his attention toward Jarrett. "I'm Margaret's father, Preston Saunders." He held out a hand.

Jarrett shook it. "Jarrett McKane. You should have let us know you were coming to town."

"This was a sudden trip for me." Saunders glanced back at his daughter. "Mia and I have been estranged for…a while."

Jarrett felt Mia stiffen. "It's been years," she insisted. "You disowned me and Brad, and you have no right to this child."

Saunders seemed surprised by his daughter's backbone. "We're still family. And this child is a Saunders which is the very reason I'm here. To help you." He glared at her. "Margaret, you can't possibly think you can give the child the kind of life he deserves." He shook his head. "You and the boy would be much better at home with your mother and me."

Mia was still trembling, even after her father left. Once the front door closed, she wanted to disappear. Instead, she hurried up the stairs to check on BJ. Anything to keep from having to face Jarrett. To have to explain. But he wasn't letting her get away, and followed her.

"Mia," he called to her.

She stopped in the upstairs hall, but didn't turn around. "I can't talk about this right now."

She started for the nursery, but he took her by the arm and led her into a guest bedroom. After the door closed, he pulled her into his arms.

She didn't resist. Shutting her eyes, she let herself revel in the secure sound of his beating heart, his warmth. She fought the tears, but lost as a sob escaped and she began to cry. She cried for the years that her parents weren't there for her. For herself because she couldn't be the daughter they wanted her to be. For the relationship she wanted with this man that now was lost too.

The only thing that mattered now was BJ.

She pulled back and wiped her eyes. "I'm sorry."

"How long since you've seen your father?" Jarrett asked as he pulled out a handkerchief and handed it to her.

"Ten years. It was a few days before my nineteenth birthday." Wiping her eyes, she raised her head. She might as well tell him everything.

"I'd just gotten released from the rehab clinic

he'd had me committed to. I was excited because he came to bring me home. Instead, he handed me five thousand dollars and said he'd paid a year's rent on an apartment in Atlanta, Georgia. He felt it would be better for everyone if I didn't return to Boston."

Mia moved across the room toward the bed. She needed space. "Funny thing was, the pills I'd become addicted to were ones prescribed by a doctor my parents insisted I see to help me lose weight."

Jarrett walked over to her. "I can't believe you were ever overweight."

"I had crooked teeth, too."

His finger touched her chin and made her look at him. "And incredible blue eyes, and hair the color of rich coffee," he told her as his gaze moved over her face. "I could go on and on."

She swallowed hard. "No one has ever said that to me."

"Maybe you never gave them a chance."

She shrugged. "I've been kind of busy lately. But Jarrett, as a teenager, I gave my father plenty of reasons not to trust me."

"Didn't we all." He smiled. "I was no angel, either. That doesn't mean you aren't a good mother now."

She gasped. "BJ." She started to leave, but he pulled her back.

"He's sleeping," Jarrett said. "You know that kid's got a strong pair of lungs, so we'll hear him when he wakes up." He paused a moment then said, "Back to you. How did you end up in Colorado?"

"I used the money my father gave me and flew to Denver. Brad was a junior pastor there. He and Karen had just gotten married, yet they opened their arms and took me in. He probably told our parents, but I think Preston was just happy I was out of his life."

"Seems that Brad wanted you," Jarrett acknowledged.

She nodded. "At first I gave him a lot of trouble. But he got me to finish high school, then college. For the first time, I felt good about myself." She felt a surge of panic. "I owe it to Brad and Karen to raise their son with love and compassion for other people. I'll do anything to keep my parents from taking BJ."

He reached for her. "It won't happen. I won't let it."

No! She couldn't let her father destroy Jarrett, too. She shook her head. "No, Jarrett, you have to stay out of this."

"Mia, listen to me. You're going to need some help."

The last thing Mia wanted was for this to go to court. She was doubtful she could win against the power of the Saunderses' money. She shook her head. "I can't let my father scare me off. I have to prove to him I can handle things on my own." She pushed past him and out the door.

More importantly, she had to get Jarrett McKane out of her life. It was the only way she could protect him.

This had been Jarrett's best Christmas in years until the unwelcome guest showed up. Although dessert was being served, he knew that for Mia the celebration was over. Using the excuse that BJ was fussy, he drove her back to town.

Mia's silence continued as they walked into the apartment building. Jarrett tugged on the glass door, hearing the scrape of metal before it gave way and opened. Inside, Jarrett glanced around the large lobby. Even with the elaborate holiday decorations, the place was still a dump.

It needed a lot of work, especially if he was going to rent to more tenants. Whether Fulton finalized the factory deal or not, he should get a contractor out here to look over the building.

Saunders must have come here first. How else would he know that Mia was at the ranch? What if he'd taken pictures? If he was going to fight for custody, would he show them to a judge?

Damn. He needed to get Mia out of here and

moved into the cottage. Honestly, he wanted her at his house, but Ms. Independence would never go for that.

At the apartment door, Mia unlocked it and they went inside. She carried the baby into the bedroom.

"I'll bring up the rest of the things," he called to her.

Jarrett hurried back outside in the cold. He opened the back of his SUV and grabbed the box of leftover food and presents. That was when he noticed the car at the end of the car park. With the help of the overhead security light, he saw the shadow of a man leaning against a dark vehicle.

He didn't like a stranger hanging around. He thought about the older tenants, then Jarrett thought about earlier today and couldn't help but wonder if Saunders had something to do with it. Had he hired someone to watch the place? Would he go that far? The man he'd met today didn't seem like the type who gave up easily.

Jarrett carried the box back inside the lobby. He took out his cell phone and called the sheriff's office, asking his old friend from high school, Danny Haskins, to come by and check out the situation. He wasn't going to make it easy for Saunders.

Call made, Jarrett returned to Mia's apartment.

When she came out of the bedroom, she didn't hide her surprise that he was there.

"Jarrett, I didn't realize you were still here."

He put the box on the table. "I brought up the rest of the things from the car."

"Oh, I'll put them away, you don't have to stay."

He was discouraged by her rejection. "Look, Mia, I saw a stranger hanging around the parking lot." He took off his hat and coat. "I'm having it checked out, so I'm not leaving here until it's cleared up. Could be your father is having someone watch you."

She looked panicked, but quickly covered it. "I have a good lock on the door. He's not getting in here."

"I want to help you."

She shook her head. "I don't want you involved in this."

He went to her. "I'm already involved, Mia."

"No, Jarrett. You can't keep rescuing me."

Before he could answer there was a knock on the door. Jarrett checked the peephole, then pulled open the door. "Hi, Danny."

The sheriff removed his hat and stepped inside the apartment. "Hey, McKane."

"Thanks for stopping by, Danny."

"Not a problem." He looked at Mia and nodded. "Hello, ma'am."

"Mia, this is Sheriff Danny Haskins. Danny, this is Mia Saunders."

"Nice to meet you, Ms. Saunders. I'm sorry to have to bother you on Christmas."

"It wasn't necessary for Jarrett to call you."

"It's my job to protect our citizens." Danny turned to Jarrett. "There was a dark sedan leaving when I pulled in, but I got the license plate. It's a rental." He pulled out a small notebook. "The name of the customer is Jake Collins of Collins Investigation. He's a P.I. out of Denver and he's been here over a week."

Haskins turned to Mia. "Jarrett told me that your father, Preston Saunders, came to Winchester Ridge after no contact with you for years."

Mia nodded. "He has a P.I. watching me to see if I make any mistakes," she said to Jarrett. "He'll use anything he can against me."

Jarrett saw not only her fear, but the sadness. Damn Saunders. "We're not going to let him," he assured her.

He walked Danny out the door. "Thanks, friend. Is there any way you could keep an eye out for this car? I'll bet my next deal that Saunders is trying to find something against his daughter so he can get custody of his grandson and it's my guess he'll do anything to get him."

"Since he isn't breaking the law, I can't do much, but I'll alert my deputies to keep an eye out. I'll also have them patrol this area." His friend smiled. "I take it you have more than a passing interest in that very attractive brunette."

"Yes, I do. So don't get any ideas."

Smiling, Danny raised a hand. "Enough said, friend. You always had all the luck when it came to the ladies. I'll let you know if I find anything."

Jarrett said goodbye, then went back inside to find Mia in the kitchen putting away leftovers.

He walked up behind her. "I don't want you to be alone tonight. I don't trust Saunders."

She closed her eyes a moment. "My father just wants me to know that he's there, that he's a threat if I don't do what he wants. I can handle this on my own."

"Like you did in the past," he said, regretting the harsh words. "Why are you being so stubborn?"

She stiffened. "Because if you stay it will only infuriate him. Believe me, you're not the type of man Preston Saunders wants his daughter to associate with. You're not successful enough, not from the right family or the right school."

"So a poor country boy isn't good enough for a Saunders?"

She glared at him. "That's correct. It's strictly eastern blueblood."

Jarrett hadn't done too badly for himself, but suddenly he felt like the kid with dirt under his fingernails.

"I'm that poor little rich girl," she told him. "I'll do whatever it takes to keep my son. So please, I need you to leave… And I mean for good."

Mia woke up the next morning, fed BJ and tried to eat but her stomach couldn't handle food. She hadn't gotten much sleep last night, either. All she kept seeing was the look on Jarrett's face.

How could she have said those things to him? The hurt she'd caused nearly killed her, but she couldn't let him get mixed up in her fight. He would lose everything.

So many things rested on her playing nice with her father. Even if she was miserable and lost the man she loved.

There was a knock on the door. She didn't open it until she heard Nola's voice.

"I was worried about you," the older woman said.

"Why? I'm just tired from the long day yesterday."

Nola watched her. "Your father showing up out of the blue might have had a lot to do with it, too."

She nodded. "I'm sorry I never told you about my parents."

Nola shook her head. "We all figured if you didn't want to talk about them you had your reasons."

Tears welled in Mia's eyes. "My father's threatening to take BJ."

Nola took hold of her hand. "He can't do that, you're a good mother. All of us can attest to that."

"But Preston Saunders has money and a legal team on his payroll that I can't compete with. He's a successful businessman, and I'm a law student who can barely make ends meet."

"What about Jarrett? He could help you."

She shook her head. "I can't let him get involved in this. You have no idea what my father could do to him. He'd destroy him without a backward glance. No, this is my fight. And I told him so last night."

Nola nodded. "That explains the man's grumpiness when I greeted him this morning. A bear, he was."

"It's better this way, Nola. He has to stay away from me."

"Why don't you let Jarrett decide if you're

worth it or not? He's a big boy. He'd probably go a few rounds with your father and still be standing afterward."

"No. This is my fight. All my life, I've let everyone else do things for me. First my parents, even Brad. Jarrett has already done too much."

"I know you can fight this. You're a strong woman who handled the tragedy of her brother's death with grace and strength. You've fought hard to get into law school. And don't you forget all the times you helped us. I remember a feisty gal who took our landlord to court so we could stay in our homes."

And fell in love with him, Mia thought. "I was only helping out my neighbors."

Nola took Mia's hands in hers. "Did you forget the most unselfish gift of all? You carried your brother's and his wife's baby."

She smiled. "Oh, Nola, that wasn't a sacrifice, that was pure joy for me. BJ is a miracle."

Nola agreed. "And no one could love him more. BJ belongs with you. What's most important, it was your brother's wish. He trusted you enough to raise his child. That should say it all. So somehow we've got to make sure that little boy stays with his mother. That's you. Nothing will ever change that."

CHAPTER TWELVE

THE next morning, Jarrett got out of bed in a bad mood. He left the apartment early so as not to run into Mia, then went in to the office, hoping to get some work done. Not possible. He couldn't clear his head of the stubborn woman.

"Ah, hell." He stood up from his desk and went to the large window looking out over the snow-covered ground. The Rocky Mountains off in the distance were magnificent against the blue sky. The view did nothing to improve his lousy mood.

How was Mia doing today? Dammit! She couldn't cave in to her father's demands. She had to stand her ground, everything would be all right. He needed to be there....

"Hey, you busy?"

Jarrett glanced over his shoulder and saw Trace peering into the office. "If I said yes, would you go away?"

He walked in. "Sorry, big brother. Your bad

attitude doesn't scare me anymore. What happened with Mia yesterday?"

It had taken a lot of years, but he finally realized that Trace and Kira wanted to be the family he'd longed for. "Nothing happened. She sent me packing last night when I offered to help her. So I don't know and I'm not sure I care."

His younger brother placed his hat on the chair and joined him at the window. "Now, that's a lie. And your way of helping is about as subtle as a bulldozer."

Jarrett glared, but Trace didn't budge. "Thanks a lot."

"I know you mean well, but it's true," Trace told him. "So what's going on with Mia's father?"

"We're pretty sure that Saunders has had a P.I. watching her this past week. He came straight out and told Mia he wants to take BJ away from her."

"What kind of a man would do that to his daughter?"

"You don't want to hear my answer to that. Besides, I told you I'm not involved in this anymore. Mia doesn't need or want my help."

"Poor Jarrett." Trace shook his head. "Ain't getting any lovin' these days."

"It isn't that way with Mia." Damn, if he didn't want it to be though. "She's a new mother."

"And a very attractive woman."

Jarrett studied his brother. "I thought you only had eyes for Kira."

"Kira has my eyes, plus my heart and soul and my fidelity. But that doesn't mean I don't notice a pretty woman. I'm not dead yet. As I remember, a while back you had eyes for my wife, too."

That seemed so long ago. Now he couldn't think of Kira as anything else but a loving sister. "Bite your tongue. She's the mother of my favorite little girl."

"I think you just found the right woman for you."

Jarrett couldn't deny it, nor could he confirm it. Mia was different from anyone he'd known.

He glanced at Trace.

"What?"

"I want to ask you something, but you'll probably think it's stupid."

"Just ask me."

"How did you know that you loved Kira?"

His brother acted surprised by the question, then he turned serious. "Honestly, I can't remember a time I didn't love her, even when our marriage was falling apart."

Trace raised his hand. "Here are a few of the symptoms if you have doubts. When Mia looks at you, you get tightness in your chest, like you can't breathe in enough air. Your heart rate isn't ever normal when she's around. And when she smiles at you." He shook his head. "It's like everything is right in the world."

Jarrett groaned. "Damn!"

There were voices in the outer office, and then his secretary, Marge, came in followed closely by Nola Madison and Joe Carson.

"Sorry, Jarrett," his secretary apologized. "I told them you were busy, but they said it's important they see you."

"It's okay, Margie." He had no idea why they would come here.

As Marge left, Nola hurried across the office. "Hello, Trace." Then she turned to him. "Jarrett, this is important. It's about Mia."

He saw the worried look on the older couple's faces. "Did something happen to her? To BJ?" He came around the desk. "Is her father causing trouble again?"

Nola looked at Joe, then turned back to him. Her large glasses made her eyes look huge. "No, she's fine for now. I would tell you, but I promised Mia I wouldn't say anything."

Jarrett frowned. "Am I supposed to guess?"

Nola shook her head. "No. I did tell Joe and Sylvia, but Sylvia is at the apartment watching BJ so Joe drove me here. He didn't promise Mia anything, so he came along to talk to you."

"Talk about what?"

Joe took over. "Mia's considering moving home with her father, so she'll be guaranteed to be a part of the boy's life."

"What? She can't do that." Jarrett started for the closet and pulled out his jacket. "How is she expected to have a life of her own? And what about BJ? We all know what Mia and Brad thought about their father's parenting skills. No, it isn't gonna happen."

Trace stopped Jarrett at the door. "Hold on there, bro. I think you need a plan before you go rushing in and playing hero."

"My plan is to stop him."

"Bulldozer," Trace reminded his brother.

"What if I tell her how I feel?"

Trace didn't look happy. "Okay. So you're ready to take the next step? The big question is, what are you going to offer her?"

Jarrett swallowed the dryness in his throat. It had been all he'd thought about it. He'd never felt about anyone the way he did about Mia. "I care about her. But you know everything is pending on this Fulton deal. I could be broke in a month."

Nola nodded. "Does that really matter? We all know the way you feel about her."

"Yeah," Joe agreed. "That was some kiss under the mistletoe."

"Thanks."

Nola pushed her way to the front. "But is it enough to commit to her?"

"Stop pushing the guy," Joe said. "He can't think."

"He doesn't have time to think about it," Nola argued. "Besides, how long does it take to know you love someone? If it's for real, you know it." The older woman turned back to Jarrett. "You know she's leaving town because of you?"

His chest tightened. "I don't want her to leave."

Joe spoke up again. "Mia's only leaving to save the factory project. Seems Mr. Saunders knows Neil Fulton and he's threatened to ruin you if she doesn't play his game."

Jarrett looked at Trace for help.

"Okay, maybe it's time we help out a little," his brother said.

Jarrett had never let anyone get this close. He thought of Mia's pretty blue eyes, her smile. Somehow she'd gotten through all his barriers. Now, nothing mattered if he couldn't be with her.

Jarrett looked at the group. "You know, this means I could be living in the apartment from now on."

Joe smiled. "Hey, Mountain View is a great place."

"Just make sure you tell that to the judge when I go back to court."

The next day, Mia walked into the hotel lobby. With each step, she had to fight the urge to turn and run. Run so far that no one would find her or BJ. She detested being here. Even as a child she'd hated that awful feeling that came when she was summoned by her father.

Nothing had changed. She was still sick to her stomach. Of course she was older and hopefully wiser. Bound and determined to stand up to the man, she had a list of rules for if she did return to Boston.

First and most important, she would never give up custody of her son. BJ would be a Saunders, but she would be his mother. So, needless to say, there were a lot of things to be ironed out before she committed to anything. She had to protect her son and herself.

She would never trust Preston Saunders. That had been the reason she left BJ with Sylvia. He wasn't getting his hands on her grandson, yet. Suddenly she was sad, thinking about leaving this town and all her friends. They'd been like family to her and BJ.

And then there was Jarrett.

She swallowed the ache in the back of her throat. She'd never wanted to hurt him, or herself, but by leaving she'd manage to do both. She knew Preston Saunders well enough to worry that he would destroy Jarrett's factory project. Perhaps even the man himself.

She also had to think about the people in town who needed those jobs created by the project. Not just in the building of the factory, but finished, it would employ a lot of workers.

She went to the desk clerk. "Preston Saunders, please."

The young man looked the name up on the computer screen. "Mr. Saunders is in one of our small conference rooms." He gave her directions.

Mia walked along the carpeted hallway and found the room. The door was ajar and she heard her father's voice. She peered in and saw that he was on his cell phone, looking out the window.

He didn't see her. "I told you it will all be taken care of by the end of the month. Yes, the money transfer will be there by the thirty-first." He nodded. "You have my word."

Mia was only half listening, but she wondered if her father could have money troubles. It wasn't a good time for a lot of businesses. She knew little about the family finances, except that both her parents came from money.

Her mother's wealth came from Ashley Oil

and Textiles. Her father's from banking. Their marriage had been more of a merger than a love match.

Since she and Brad had been disinherited, she didn't concern herself with any of that. She only cared about BJ. And she would do anything to keep him. Even sell her soul.

Preston ended his call and turned around to see her. "Eavesdropping isn't polite, Margaret."

She walked up to the table. "You're the one who set up this meeting. Besides, you're the one who's been sneaking around. I don't think I want to stay if you're going to be condescending."

She started to leave and he called her back. With hesitation, she turned around and waited.

"Maybe we both got off on the wrong foot," he said.

"That's what you call destroying my life?"

"I want to be a part of my grandson's life. Is that so awful?"

"You keep saying that." She paused. "What about Mother? Is she here with you?"

He shook his head. "No, your mother stayed home. She didn't want to get her hopes up if this didn't work out."

Mia had realized a long time ago that Abigail was just what Preston wanted her to be. A society wife. She did charity events, but raising her children was just too difficult for her. Nannies had always taken care of her and Brad. Mia was afraid that would happen with BJ. She couldn't let history repeat itself. She reached inside her purse, took out an envelope and handed to her father.

"What's this?"

"The list of conditions you have to agree to if you want me to return to Boston."

"You're in no position to demand anything."

She straightened her back. "If you don't want a court battle, Father, we need to come to terms. I will never hand over my son to you. I'm BJ's mother and that isn't going to change." She still needed to work out the legal adoption agreement. "So we're working on my terms. You've got twenty-four hours to give me an answer."

She swung around and marched out, praying he wouldn't stop her. She'd crumble for sure. But just thinking of BJ gave her strength. He was all she had. She'd lost everyone else, she couldn't lose him, too.

Later that day, Trace and Jarrett were at the office doing research on Preston Saunders. Thanks to his Internet whiz, Margie, they'd been able to learn a lot about the Saunders family, including the fact that Saunders Investments was a Fortune 500 company.

"How much to do you want to bet Mia is a shareholder?" Jarrett glanced at Trace. "I wouldn't put it past Preston to have another reason besides his grandson for showing up here. Could it have something to do with money? Mia's money?"

"Wait, this is all speculation," Trace said.

"You didn't talk to this man—I did," Jarrett assured him. "By Mia's own admission, he's been a lousy father. And on Christmas, he made no bones about trying to use his authority over his daughter by showing up and trying to regain that control and take his grandson. There's got to be a reason why he's here." He stood. "And I'm going to find out what it is."

"Where are you headed?"

"To see Mia. Whether she likes it or not."

That evening, Mia was still shaken from the visit with her father. Of course, this time she'd done a lot of the talking, but he'd definitely had enough to say.

She looked down and watched the baby at her breast and smiled. She began to calm down. No way did she want to relay her anxiety to BJ.

She knew Preston would be upset with her demands. She'd insisted she have her own apartment, refusing to live in the large house she was raised in. She refused to let her father control her life again. But as long as she had BJ, life would be good.

She heard a knock on the apartment door. "Come in, Nola, it's unlocked," she called from the bedroom.

When she looked up, she saw Jarrett standing in the doorway of her bedroom.

"It's not Nola," he told her.

She tried to cover herself, but BJ was having none of it. He began to fuss. She raised him to her shoulder and quickly made an adjustment to rearrange her blouse.

"Jarrett, I'm busy right now. So if you'll—"

He walked toward the bed. "Leave?" he finished for her. "I will, but first we need to talk, Mia. And we need to be honest."

Mia stared at the man. He looked so good she felt a stirring that made her ache. "We've said everything already."

"No, we haven't." He sat down on the bed. "Look, Mia, I know why you're doing this. It's because of what your father threatened to do to me."

She couldn't answer him. "Who told you that? Did my father say something to you?"

He shook his head. "I wish he had, because I'd have let him know that he couldn't scare me off."

She rubbed the baby's back as he squirmed

in her arms. "That's not it. I decided that I need my family around me. It'll be good for BJ."

He leaned closer. "You have family here, too." Those dark eyes held hers. "You deserve a good life, Mia. I don't believe you'll have that if Preston is running the show."

"I just want to keep my son."

BJ let out a cry.

"Seems the little guy isn't happy," Jarrett said and reached for the baby. "Let me."

Before Mia could stop him, he'd lifted the infant off her shoulder, but Jarrett's focus was still on Mia. She quickly pulled her blouse together, covering her exposed breast.

He put the baby against his shoulder and began to pat his back. He spoke in a soothing voice and, after a burp, the baby calmed down. He returned him to Mia's outstretched arms.

"He should be able to finish his supper now."

Jarrett's gaze held hers and she couldn't look away, nor did she want to. They'd shared so many things in the past few months. He'd been a part of BJ's life from the beginning. She opened her blouse, moved her son to her other breast, and he began to nurse again.

Jarrett drew an audible breath. "I don't think I've ever seen anything so beautiful."

She looked at him, feeling tears building

in her eyes. "Please, don't do this. It's hard enough..."

He placed a finger against her lips. "It's going to be okay, Mia. I promise you." He leaned down and brushed his mouth against hers. She sucked in a breath and he came back for more. The slow, lingering kiss wasn't enough, but she couldn't take any more.

With a shuddering sigh he pulled back. "I don't want to let you go."

She swallowed hard. "Oh, Jarrett, there's not a choice."

"There's always a choice, Mia," Jarrett told her and stepped back, away from temptation. "Now, to return to why I stopped by— I believe your father's sudden appearance has to do with money, your money and your brother's money."

She looked confused. "We don't have any money."

"You're listed as a stockholder in the family business."

"No, he took the money away from us when we left home."

"Your father doesn't run Ashley Oil and Textiles. Your maternal grandfather, Clyde Ashley, began that family business. Did you know your grandfather?"

She shook her head. "Not really, I was five when he died."

"It's only speculation, I'm going to bet Clyde had made provisions for his grandchildren in his will. Did you or Brad ever get any money from him?"

"We never wanted anything from the family."

"I understand, but you're entitled to it, Mia. More importantly, you could use it for BJ and his future. And if your brother had his trust coming, it would definitely go to his son."

Mia's eyes rounded as things started falling into place. "That's why Preston wants BJ?"

As if the baby heard his name, he paused and looked up at his mother. She smoothed her hand over his head, and coaxed him back to her breast.

Jarrett glanced away a moment to gather his thoughts away from Mia. How incredibly beautiful she looked with her child. "Have you noticed any correspondence concerning insurance policies, or where your brother's financial records might be?"

"I've already collected Brad's insurance. Every other piece of paperwork that my brother had I put in a file box." She raised BJ to her shoulder and began to pat his back. "It's in the hall closet." This time, BJ burped like a pro.

She got up and carried the infant to the crib. Buttoning her blouse, she went to the hall and retrieved the box.

She carried it to the coffee table in the living room. "I put everything in here after the accident. If it didn't need to be paid, I didn't really look at it."

"You had enough to deal with." He arched an eyebrow. "Do you mind if I have a look now?"

Mia shook her head. She would do anything that might stop her father.

She watched as Jarrett shuffled through the file for a few minutes, then he extracted an envelope and took out the letter. He scanned it. "Bingo. I think I found it."

Jarrett handed the paper to her. The letterhead was that of a law firm, Knott, Lewis and Johnston. It was from James Knott, addressed to Brad and dated a year earlier.

The lawyer said that he was the executor of Clyde Ashley's estate. Since Bradley had reached his thirty-fifth birthday he was now entitled to his inheritance. No amount was given. Just to contact him as soon as possible, and a phone number.

Mia was in shock. "Why hadn't Bradley gone to claim his money?"

Jarrett shrugged. "Maybe he didn't have a chance."

Mia thought back. "He turned thirty-five not long before his and Karen's trip to Mexico. Maybe he was going to contact the lawyer when he returned home."

"And he never got the chance," Jarrett finished. "Maybe the lawyer contacted your father and that sent Preston searching and he found out about his son's death. And since no one has kept it a secret that BJ is Brad's child, your father learned about a grandson."

That didn't stop Mia's worry. "So now he's going to try and have me proved an unfit mother to get the money. He doesn't have enough?"

"And we can't let him have it. This money will secure BJ's future."

"Not if he proves I'm a bad mother."

"Hey, where's that feisty woman who came after me? Mia, you're a great mother. Besides, you've got the most important thing on your side—your brother wanted you to raise his son. So much so, he put it in writing."

CHAPTER THIRTEEN

LATER that afternoon Jarrett paced his office. Mia was on her way to the hotel to see her father, while Fulton was on his way here to discuss his board of directors' decision about the factory project.

Hell. He didn't want to think about business right now.

What he wanted was Mia as far away from Preston Saunders as possible. That wasn't going to happen today. He'd wanted to go with her, but she'd insisted that she needed to confront the man by herself. Her only concession had been to let Nola go to help watch BJ.

Still Jarrett didn't trust Saunders. He wouldn't put it past him to kidnap them both and drag them back to Connecticut.

"The hell with this." He headed for the door just as Neil Fulton walked into the outer office.

"Hey, Jarrett. How was your holiday?"

"It was busy. And yours?"

Neil seemed to be in a good mood. "The same. I didn't know if I could get away early. I'm glad we could get together on such short notice."

"About that, Neil. An emergency has come up and I need to leave."

The man frowned. "I'm sorry. Can I help?"

Jarrett wasn't planning to mention Saunders but what did he have to lose? He didn't care about the project unless he had Mia. "Maybe you can. I hear you're a friend of Preston Saunders, but the guy's a real bastard."

"Whoa, whoa." Neil raised a hand. "Who told you we were friends? I've only met him a few times at fundraisers."

Jarrett was puzzled. "Aren't your wives sorority sisters?"

He nodded. "They went to the same eastern college, but that doesn't mean they're friends. There's no connection between us, I haven't seen the man in probably five years." Neil frowned. "Rumor has it he's lost a bundle on sub-prime mortgage loans."

Jarrett cursed, and filled Fulton in on the details of what had been going on since Saunders came to town. "He said he'd talked to you about putting a halt to the factory project."

Neil shook his head. "Even if Saunders and I

were friends, I would never let personal issues interfere with my business decisions. It never works out. Although I do listen to my wife, and she's definitely a fan of yours. She likes a man with integrity. You didn't toss your tenants out on the street, even though it could mean losing this deal."

"Yeah, even I have a heart."

"That's not always a bad thing. It actually helped you win this deal. Several of the board members are inclined to agree with my Robin." Neil smiled. "She's looking forward to meeting you."

Jarrett blinked. "Meeting me? You've decided to build the factory here?"

Neil nodded. "You were right, your location is the best and there's plenty of room to expand. And as long as the business offices are going into your retro apartment building, Robin wants to help decorate them."

Jarrett knew he was grinning like a fool. "I'll have it put into the contract. Could we talk about this later?" He slipped on his coat. "I need to let someone know I want to be a part of her future. And boot a certain someone else out of town."

"Would you like some backup? I wouldn't mind helping bring Saunders down."

"It could get nasty."

Neil straightened. "I can hold my own. I want to see you get the girl, too."

"Not as much as I do."

Mia pushed BJ's stroller into the hotel. She hadn't wanted to come back here again, but she didn't want her father anywhere near her apartment.

All she wanted was to finish this for good. She wanted Preston out of her life. More importantly, out of her son's life.

No matter what it cost financially.

"Mia, I wish you would think about this for a few days," Nola said as she walked alongside her. "I don't trust the man. You shouldn't, either. Maybe you should call Jarrett."

Two months ago she hadn't even known Jarrett McKane. And now she was hopelessly in love with the guy. She thought about all the things he'd done for her, for BJ. How he'd been there for her when she'd really needed him. He'd coached her through her son's birth. When she was exhausted, he walked the floor with BJ so she could sleep.

"Nola, I can't let Jarrett suffer at my father's hand. This is my problem. I should've stood up to my father years ago, but this is going to end today." She couldn't let Jarrett lose everything because of her. Not for her past sins.

That was the reason she'd just give Preston what he wanted. Money. Then he would leave town, and she and BJ could have a peaceful, loving life.

"I know Jarrett doesn't mind helping you." The older woman walked next to the stroller. "You have to know he cares about you and BJ."

"Yes, he's been a good friend." She wanted more.

"Friend?" The older woman gave her a sideways glance. "I think you'd better open your eyes and see how that man looks at you. Even you can't be that blind."

No, she wasn't blind. "Okay, I've seen him watching me." They continued along the hall to the small conference room. "But Jarrett McKane watches a lot of women."

"All men look—until they find the right one. You're Jarrett's right one, Mia. Don't let your father spoil your chance at happiness. Jarrett is a good man." Nola smiled. "He reminds me a lot of Reverend Brad," she rushed on. "Maybe Jarrett has a slightly rougher side, and he curses a little too much, but he has the same good heart."

Mia stopped. "I know all this Nola. It's one of the reasons I'm doing this."

Her friend pursed her lips and shook her head.

"I don't need the money. What Jarrett's doing for this town by creating jobs is much more important. I can work. I plan to finish school and make a good life for BJ. I won't ever let my father hurt the people I care about."

Mia released a breath, and pushed the stroller through the conference-room door to see her father standing by the window. Dressed in his tailored gray suit, he took his time to come to greet her.

"Margaret."

She gripped the stroller handle tighter. "Hello, Father."

He nodded and turned to Nola. "We haven't had the pleasure."

"Nola Madison, Mr. Saunders. I'm a *very* good friend of Mia's."

Mia watched her father look down at the stroller, studying the sleeping child, but he didn't comment on his grandson. "Maybe we should get started."

"Yes," Mia agreed. "We have a lot to cover before you leave town."

At the front desk, Jarrett and Neil got directions to the conference room and headed across the lobby. Their pace picked up when he saw Nola with BJ in the stroller.

"Oh, Jarrett," she cried. "I'm so glad you're here."

"Of course I'm here. Nola, this is Neil Fulton. Neil, Nola Madison. He's going to help us."

The two exchanged pleasantries, then Jarrett nodded toward the door. "Is Mia inside?"

"Yes, she's with her father. I'm worried, Jarrett, she's trying to protect everyone but herself." The baby started to fuss, and Nola rocked the stroller. "See, even BJ's upset."

Jarrett directed Nola to a lounge area a short distance away, and promised her everything would turn out okay. Then he partially opened the conference-room door to hear what was going on. He saw the father and daughter across the small room, their backs to him.

"You can't have BJ," Mia insisted. "And I'm not returning to Boston with you, either."

"You're making a big mistake, Margaret. I hate to go to court and spill all the family secrets, but you know I will. I have to protect my grandson."

"And I have to protect my son from you. Come on, we're alone, you can admit you only want BJ because of Bradley's trust fund."

Saunders tried to act wounded and failed. "How could you accuse me of something like that? Besides, you should know that any money would stay in trust for Bradley's son. I couldn't get my hands on it."

"As the child's guardian, you'd have access to the account. It must be a sizable amount for you to come all this way."

"I can't touch it. Your grandfather made the trust airtight." He studied her. "You, on the other hand…you have something I want."

After all this time, she'd thought she was immune to his ability to hurt her. She wasn't. "What is that?"

"Your grandfather Ashley was very generous to you in his will. Not only with a trust fund, but with company stock. You can't touch the money until you're thirty-five or married. But there is the question of the stock."

"You want my Ashley Oil stock?"

"I've earned it. I've been voting your shares for years."

"How? You shouldn't have had access once I turned twenty-one."

He smiled. "You don't remember signing power of attorney over to me? When you got out of rehab?"

She hated to think about that time of her life. She did remember her signature had been her ticket out. All she had to do was give Preston Saunders what he wanted, and she'd get her freedom. "So what else could you want?"

"Your grandfather was overprotective. I only had a temporary power of attorney and it's expired."

After all these years, her father had only tracked her down to get money from her. "Why don't I just hold out my arm and you can take all my blood, too."

"Don't act so dramatic. For years, your mother and I had to explain away your indiscretions."

She wasn't going to let him bring her down. "I was your daughter," she stressed, then calmed down. "You never once accepted me for who I was. When I had a problem, you were never there for me.

"You had the Saunders name and money, more advantages than a lot of kids. So it was expected you'd do well. Bradley Junior will have to do the same."

"No, you won't do the same thing to my son."

Preston glared at her. "He's not your son, Margaret. He's your nephew. And he needs to be raised as a Saunders."

"Never," she insisted. BJ was hers. She'd already started legal procedures.

Jarrett watched Mia stand tough. Yet, Preston wasn't relenting, either. "I changed my mind on one of the conditions of our new agreement. Along with your stock, I want to see my grandson periodically. Say, four times a year. And I'll need the stock signed over immediately."

She shook her head. "That's not our deal. You get the money. You walk away."

"You're not dictating to me. Secrets could leak out. There's a certain factory project that hangs in the balance."

Jarrett couldn't stand back any longer. He glanced at Neil as he swung open the door and walked into the room.

Preston Saunders was the first to notice him. "So you brought your cowboy along to save you."

Mia turned around. He could see her shock and some relief. "Jarrett. What are you doing here?"

He came up to her. "I thought you might need some support."

"I don't want you involved in this. I can handle it."

He leaned closer and whispered, "Woman, as far as I'm concerned, you could handle anything. But if you think I'm going to stand by and let this guy hurt you, you'd better think again." He gave her a quick kiss, then placed his arm around her shoulders and faced the problem.

"Your words are touching, Mr. McKane," her father said, "but this doesn't concern you."

"I think it does, Mr. Saunders. I don't like that you've threatened Mia."

"As I said, this doesn't concern you." He looked at Mia. "Does it, Margaret?"

She looked at Jarrett. "He's right. This isn't good for the factory project."

"You think I care about the project more than you?" He smiled. "I can't tell you how much it means to me that you're willing to sacrifice your future for me. But there's no need."

He turned to Preston. "Okay, Saunders, here's how it's going to be. You're going to leave town *today*. Mia is going to stay here, finish law school and raise her son. Oh, and if I'm lucky, I get to be a part of their lives."

"Well, you're going to have to live off her money, because your future is looking bleak at the moment. You're about to lose everything."

"I think you're wrong about that, Saunders."

Everyone turned toward the door as Neil Fulton walked in. He went to stand beside Jarrett and Mia.

"Neil," her father stammered. "It's good to see you again."

"I don't think so, Saunders. First thing, I don't like you tossing my name around as if we're friends." He glared at Preston. "Secondly, Jarrett McKane and my company just agreed on a rather lucrative property deal. Nothing you say is going to change a thing." He took a step closer to Preston. "So I suggest you do what Jarrett asked, because I also heard you threaten your daughter. And believe me, you don't want to mess with me."

Her father looked at Mia. "Margaret, are you going to allow this?"

Mia knew he wouldn't stop trying to control her. "Yes." She fought tears that it had to come to this. "Please don't contact me again."

If Preston was surprised, he hid it. "Your mother is going to be so disappointed."

"Please tell Mother that she's more than welcome to visit her grandson."

Preston Saunders started for the door, but stopped and looked back at her. "I wouldn't act so smug if I were you, Margaret, not with your past. There's a lot of things that could come out I'm sure you'd like to keep buried." He nodded to Jarrett. "I'm sure your friends would be interested to know their sweet Mia isn't so innocent." He turned and walked out the door.

Mia felt the heat climb to her face and those dark years came rushing back, threatening to consume her, take away everything she'd made good in her life.

"Mia, are you okay?"

She nodded and put on a smile.

Neil looked at Jarrett. "I think I'll leave you

two alone to talk." He turned to Mia. "It's a pleasure to meet you, Mia. I hope we get a chance to talk later." With a nod, Neil Fulton walked out, leaving her with Jarrett.

She looked at him, saw his questioning look, then burst into tears and ran out of the room, too.

Two hours later, Mia was back at her apartment. She fed BJ, and, after putting him down to nap, she dragged her suitcase from the closet and began to pack.

Okay, she was a coward. But when it came to a protecting her son, she'd do anything, go anywhere. She wasn't sure if her father would bring her past out in court. Would he even take her to court?

Mia sank to the sofa. After all these years, all the things she'd accomplished, she'd turned her life around, and still her past had caught up with her. And she couldn't trust anyone to love her if they found out the truth about her.

She brushed away a tear. "Brad, I wish you were here to help me."

She stood and looked around. There wasn't much worth taking with her, except the baby things. She needed some boxes and went to the stairwell to get some. She found two. As she returned to her apartment, Trace McKane got off the elevator. She couldn't avoid him.

He smiled. "Hey, Mia. Have you seen Jarrett?"

She shook her head. "Not since earlier."

Trace played with his cowboy hat in his hands. "I hear you talked with your father. I hope that went well."

"He's leaving town, and I hope it's the end of it." She motioned to her apartment. "I'd better get inside to BJ."

He glanced at the boxes as he walked with her. "So you're getting ready to move out to the cottage? Maybe I can take some things out today."

She couldn't make eye contact as she backed up to her apartment door. "Look, Trace, I appreciate you and Kira offering us a place to live, but I've decided to move back to Denver for school."

Before Trace could say anything, the sound of BJ's cry distracted them. She hurried inside and got her son back to sleep, then returned to the living room. Trace was waiting.

"I know it isn't any of my business, but are you leaving because of my brother?"

She shook her head. "No, it's me. I feel it's for the best."

He watched her. "I'm not buying it. I know

you have feelings for Jarrett, and the guy's crazy about you. What's the real reason?"

She couldn't deny it. She was totally in love with Jarrett. "I don't think it will work out. My father will probably try and cause more trouble." She glanced away. "There are things in my past." She shook her head. "A time in my life when I didn't care much about myself. I did things I'm not proud of."

"All of us have those times. Jarrett and I have a lot of bad history. We really haven't been brothers until the last few years." He studied her. "And Kira and I had our share of rough times, too. It took her years to tell me she'd had a baby when she was fifteen. She gave him up."

Mia remembered Jenna saying she had an older brother. "That must have been hard for her."

He nodded. "I was married to her and she never told me. When I finally found out, of course I was hurt. Not over what she did at fifteen and alone, but because she didn't trust me enough to tell me. We almost split up over it."

She couldn't imagine Trace and Kira not together. "I just have so much baggage. I can't keep dumping it on Jarrett."

Trace smiled. "Do you see the man complaining? He's crazy about you and BJ. Besides,

Jarrett isn't an angel, either. There's plenty of women around town that will attest to that."

She wasn't sure what to say, then suddenly she blurted out. "I love him too much to hurt him."

He turned serious. "A few years ago, I would have told you to walk away from Jarrett, that you were too good for him. But he's changed. Give him a chance to prove that he's the man you need."

By about five that night, Jarrett wasn't sure what he was doing. Things hadn't turned out as he'd planned. He'd charged in to help, but in the end he didn't get the girl.

He knew that talking with her father had taken its toll on Mia. But he also thought that she'd rush into his arms when it was over. Instead, she'd run out the door, right out of his life.

He'd tried calling her several times, but she didn't answer. How could he tell her how he felt in a phone message?

After Mia's rejection, he'd spent the day with Neil going over the changes in the project. That was the reason he'd called this meeting of the tenants. They were going to be a big part of this and he wanted to make sure everyone agreed to his proposal.

He'd hoped to see Mia when he walked into

the community room, but she wasn't there. As he made his way to the front, the room grew quiet and everyone turned to him.

"Good evening, everyone." He glanced around, realizing how many of the tenants he'd gotten to know these past months. He'd shared meals and holidays with these people.

"I know you've all wondered why I called this meeting. Well, as of a few hours ago, I finalized and signed the contracts for the new factory to be built. So the construction is scheduled to start in the early spring." The tenants exchanged glances, but didn't say anything. "Since we last gathered, there have been some changes to the plans. Neil Fulton has agreed to build further back on the property. I feel this is a better solution for all of us."

"You mean for you," someone said.

"Just hear me out." He took a breath. "First of all, when I say the factory will be relocated on the back of the property that means the apartment buildings won't be torn down. Instead, the vacant building will be used to house Fulton's corporate offices, and this building will be remodeled and left as Mountain View Apartments."

Jarrett raised his hand to quiet the suddenly noisy group. "Of course, there's going to be a lot of construction noise during the remodeling.

So I'm going to compensate you all with lower rents for the next six months."

Joe stood. "Wait, we don't have to move out by March?"

"No. Unless you want to. But it's a better investment for me to keep the building open. We're in an era of recycling, so I want to bring these apartments back to their original state by painting and repairing the structure. The kitchens and baths will be updated, of course, with new appliances and fixtures. So what I need to know is, how do you feel about continuing to live here?"

Cheers went up in the room.

Joe got out of his chair again. "How much more will it cost us in rent?"

"Since you all lived here at the worst time, you shouldn't have to pay any extra once things improve. So there won't be any increase in rent for any of the tenants living here now."

"We'll need to get it writing," a familiar voice called out from the back of the room.

Heart pounding, Jarrett looked toward the doorway. Mia was standing there behind BJ's stroller. She looked tired, but as beautiful as usual.

"I can do that," he offered. "Anything else you need?"

Mia didn't take her eyes off Jarrett as she

moved along the side of the tables. She had so many things she needed to say to him. Maybe this wasn't the place, but she had to see him. She had to give this one last chance. For both of them.

"A good handyman on the premises," she went on. "Someone who can take care of emergencies." Nola came over, took the stroller as Mia continued to the front of the room. She stopped in front of Jarrett. "Someone we can count on."

He studied her for a moment and nodded. "Do you think you'll need someone just during the day or around the clock?"

Those dark eyes locked on hers, and she wondered if he could read her mind, her heart. She could barely speak. "Oh, definitely around the clock. Do you know of anyone?"

"Yeah, I've got just the guy for the job." He took a step forward and she could feel everyone in the room hanging on their words.

"Does he like children?"

Jarrett didn't even blink. "He loves children." Then he smiled. "And pets." He inched closer. "Does this suit you, Ms. Saunders?"

She could only manage a nod.

"Maybe we should go somewhere and discuss this further."

"Just kiss her," someone yelled.

A smile appeared across Jarrett's face. "I'm also good at taking directions."

His head lowered to hers and he captured her mouth. This time whistles and cheers erupted. He kept it light, but he told her everything she needed to know. They might just have a chance.

CHAPTER FOURTEEN

JARRETT wasn't exactly crazy about having an audience when he was trying to talk to Mia. That was the reason he'd hurried her and BJ out of there and into his SUV.

He ended up taking Mia to his house. Guaranteed privacy. He pulled in to his long driveway, opened the garage and drove in. Once the door shut behind the car, he reached for her hand.

"We need to talk without being interrupted." He brushed his lips across hers, then got out, took BJ out of the back and they walked inside through the kitchen.

He looked down at the sleeping baby. "How soon before he needs to be fed?"

"We have a few hours."

"Good." He took her into the living room, only the outside light on the patio illuminating the space. Setting the baby's carrier down on the rug at one end of the sofa, he turned on the gas fireplace and some soft music.

"I haven't been home much lately," he told her. "I don't have much to offer you."

"I don't want anything."

He moved to turn on a lamp.

"Please leave it off," she asked. "It's nice like this. It's peaceful and the view is incredible."

With a nod, he took her hand and they sat down on the sofa. For a long time, they stared out the French doors watching the wintry scene. The snow on the ground lightened the area, illuminating the rows of bare trees that dotted the landscape.

He began. "Tell me I haven't messed up everything by coming after you today."

Mia squeezed his hand, trying to relay how she felt. She couldn't look at him. Her father had nearly destroyed a lot of people and maybe the future of the town. "No. I'm just sorry you got caught in this mess."

"I don't care about your past, Mia. Meeting your father explained a lot to me. I came to the hotel to support you. When Nola told me the truth about what your father had threatened, I couldn't stand by and let him blackmail you."

"It's only money," she insisted. "I don't care about that. It's BJ I care about. I just didn't want my son raised the way Brad and I were. In a house without love."

"You should have told your father to take a hike. My failure on the project would have saved the apartments."

"I couldn't do that. You've worked too hard on bringing the factory to town. I didn't want my father to destroy you." She took another risk and confessed, "I care about you."

He reached for her, and she didn't resist as he turned her in his arms so she was facing him. He pressed her head against his chest and she could feel the rapid beating of his heart.

"And I care about you," he informed her. Not just you, but BJ, too." He touched her face, tilting her head back so she had to look at him.

"I more than care, Mia. I love you."

Her breathing caught as her throat tightened with emotions. She couldn't speak.

"Crazy, huh?" He placed a soft kiss on her forehead, then on one eyelid, then the other. "I don't know how or when it happened, I'm thinking the second I saw you." He continued kissing his way down her cheek. "All I know is I couldn't seem to stay away. I used every excuse I could to see you." He placed a kiss against her ear and she shivered, resting her hand against his solid chest, trying to resist. "Then all those precious moments—when we shared the ultrasound of the baby, BJ's birth."

Every word he spoke made her yearn for more. She wanted everything from this man. "I'm glad you were there with me, too."

He ran his mouth over her jaw. "All I know is that when I thought you were leaving, I couldn't let you go."

She gasped. "Oh, Jarrett," she breathed, her body responding to his touch.

He raised his head. "Hey, I'm pouring out my heart here and that's all you have to say."

Tears filled her eyes. "I love you, too."

"You don't sound happy about it." He sat her up, stood and walked to the French door. "Maybe I've read the wrong signals here."

She hated seeing his hurt, but she wasn't sure she could handle his rejection. She went to him. "You might change your mind when you learn about the things I've done."

"We've all done things. So you were hooked on prescription drugs, you already told me that. It's not a problem now, is it?"

She shook her head. "I didn't tell you all of it. There was more."

He waited for her to speak.

"I ran with a wild crowd in high school. You know how bored rich kids go out partying?

We drank so to forget our rotten lives. A joke, huh?"

"Not after meeting Preston."

Here was the hard part for her. "I had a drinking problem, Jarrett. My father was right, he helped me get out of several messes. The worst was one night when I left a party so drunk I ran my car into a tree. I wasn't hurt, but my passenger was."

"How bad was he hurt?"

"Thank God, it was nothing permanent, but he was in the hospital for a while. My father rescued me, paid off his family and the local police. Otherwise I might have gone to jail and have a police record, not be working on becoming a lawyer."

"How old were you?"

"Seventeen."

"I was nineteen when I was stopped for drinking and driving. And because I was the local football star, I got off, too." He took a step closer to her. "We were kids, Mia. We were given a second chance. What happened after that?"

"Even that scare didn't stop me. That's when my father put me into rehab and I finally got sober."

"How long?"

"It's been ten years." She released a breath. "I can't drink alcohol, Jarrett."

"Do you feel the need to?"

"I haven't for a while, maybe when Brad died, and then when my father came to town..." She stopped. "I need to go back to meetings. It's been a while."

The last thing Jarrett had expected was to hear Mia say she was an alcoholic. His chest tightened as he tried to imagine what she had gone through. Her brother had been her only support. Now he wanted to be. "If you'd like, I'll go with you."

She blinked and a tear fell. "Why, Jarrett?"

"I've been trying to tell you, Mia Saunders. I love you. But for some crazy reason, you think you don't deserve that. I guess I'm just going to have to prove it to you."

Jarrett lowered his head and captured her mouth. He swiftly deepened the kiss, drinking in her sweetness that made him so hungry for more. He ran his hands over her body, folding his palm over her lush breast. She moaned and moved against him.

He broke off the kiss on a ragged breath. "Nothing matters but this. Not your past nor mine. It's how I feel when you're close to me. How wonderful it's going to be when we finally make love. I love you, Mia."

She touched his jaw. "I love you too."

He smiled against her mouth. "Now those are

the words that get my attention. And I never get tired of hearing them." He kissed her again, and again, until he was desperate for her. "I want you, Mia."

She drew a needed breath. "I want to make love with you, too, Jarrett, but I can't—"

"I know it's too soon." He leaned his forehead against her and groaned. "It's killing me, but I can wait."

She laid her head against his chest. "I may die before then," she added, enjoying him touching her.

"Then we'd better get married fast."

Jarrett felt her tense and she pulled back. "You want to get married?"

He swallowed. "Did I forget to mention that?"

She nodded.

"I guess I should be more direct." Of course, he hadn't exactly been prepared for this moment. He didn't even have a ring. Then he remembered his mother's.

"Just give me a second." He gave her a quick kiss and hurried off down the hall to his bedroom. He opened the top drawer of his dresser, digging through some things until he found the keepsake box he had since he'd been a kid.

Inside was a ring, a small sapphire circled in

tiny diamonds. It had belonged to his mother and she gave it to him before she died.

It probably wasn't worth much by today's standards. But it meant a lot to him. He returned and saw Mia standing by the French doors.

He came up behind her and hugged her. "Are you planning your escape?"

She shook her head. "I love it here. It must be wonderful to live out here."

He hadn't realized how wonderful until he'd seen it through her eyes. "I saved five acres before I sold the rest of my share of the ranch to Trace. So neighbors aren't too close."

"I'm glad, and if we have neighbors, it's your family."

He turned her toward him. "Do you want to live out here, Mia?"

She rose up on her toes and kissed him. "Anywhere you are, Jarrett McKane."

That was all he needed. He went down on his knee. "I love you, Mia Saunders. You'd make me so happy if you'll agree to be my wife."

"Yes, oh, Jarrett, yes. I'll marry you."

He stood and took the ring out of his pocket. "It belonged to my mother," he told her as he slipped it on her finger. It was too big. "We can get you something else."

"No, all I want is to have this sized, then it'll be perfect."

He kissed her, sweetly and tenderly. "I have one more request. I'd like to adopt BJ. I don't want to replace his real father, but it's important that we're a true family. I don't want him ever to feel left out, or that he doesn't belong."

"I think Brad would like that." She kissed him. "You're a good man, Jarrett. How lucky BJ and I are to have you."

"I think we make a great team," he said, knowing they were getting what they all wanted—to be a family.

Mia began to look around. "Just think how wonderful this house will look decorated for the holidays."

Jarrett drew her back into his arms. "As long as there is plenty of mistletoe, I'll be happy."

EPILOGUE

It was January.

A new year, a new beginning, but not before he closed one last chapter of his life. Today Jarrett returned to court and Judge Gillard. He hoped it was for the last time. He glanced at his soon-to-be bride next to him. In three days, she would be his wife, and soon after that, he hoped BJ would be his son.

"It's going to be okay," she whispered. "The judge will be happy with the way things turned out."

He thought so too, but he loved having her positive reinforcement.

Suddenly the court was called to order by the deputy, and Judge Gillard walked up behind the bench and sat in her chair. She glanced over her first file, then looked at Jarrett.

"Case number 4731," the deputy began, "Mountain View Apartment tenants vs. Jarrett McKane."

"Here, your honor," Jarrett said.

"We're here, too, your honor," Mia said and glanced back at Nola, Joe and Sylvia who'd come today, too. Trace and Kira were there too, holding BJ. Sometimes, Jarrett found it hard to believe they were rooting him on.

"Your honor," Mia began. "We'd like to drop the charges against Mr. McKane."

The judge looked over her glasses at Mia. "It's too late for that. I gave Mr. McKane a job to do, and for his sake, I hope it's been completed."

"It has been, your honor," Jarrett said. "I have the sign-off from code enforcement, saying everything was completed as asked."

The judge glanced over the sheet, then looked at Mia. "Are the tenants happy with the results?"

Mia smiled. "Very much so. Right now, Mr. McKane is in the process of remodeling the property."

The judge frowned as she turned to Jarrett. "I thought the building was going to be torn down."

"There's been a change," he told her. "With a slight modification to the building plans, the apartments are no longer interfering with the factory construction. So I've decided to keep it as an investment."

Judge Gillard leaned back in her chair and

studied him for a moment. Then she turned to Mia. "Is everyone happy about the situation?"

Nola stood up. "May I speak, your honor?"

"It's Mrs. Madison, isn't it?," the judge asked, then, at Nola's nod, she waved her up to the front. "Please, tell us how you feel."

Nola came up next to Jarrett. "It's been wonderful. We're all getting new apartments and Jarrett isn't even going to raise our rent. We're getting a new neighbor, too. Fulton Industries is opening their business office in the other building, and Mr. Fulton said that maybe some of us can work there part-time." She smiled. "This is all thanks to Jarrett McKane, your honor. He gave us a home when no one else cared. Now he's our friend and he's going to marry Mia and be a father to her baby."

The judge looked overwhelmed. "Well, that's more information than I needed," she said. "But I'm glad it all has worked out for everyone."

She looked at Jarrett. "When is the wedding?"

"Excuse me?"

"The wedding?"

Jarrett caught Mia's attention. "This Saturday at the First Community Church, one o'clock. The reception afterward is in the Mountain View's community room. You're welcome to come, your honor. You did play a big part in getting us together."

She gave him a half smile. "Glad I could help. I might surprise you and show up. I wouldn't mind checking out an apartment for my mother. I like how everyone at Mountain View watches out for each other."

"We do," Jarrett assured her. "And there's a full-time handyman and around-the-clock security on the premises. We'll have some vacancies in another month. Joe and Sylvia Carson are going to be the managers."

Joe stood and waved to the judge.

"I'll have to look into it," she said and glanced over the paper again. "Well, it looks like everything is in order."

Barbara Gillard eyed the couple. "I wish all my cases ended like this. Congratulations," she said and smiled. "I guess there's nothing more to say. "Case dismissed."

The following Saturday evening, Mia sat beside Jarrett in the SUV as they left the wedding reception that had been filled with friends and family. Now they drove toward their home. She couldn't believe it, just a few hours ago they'd got married.

"Have I told you how beautiful you looked today?"

"Yes, but I like hearing it."

"You look beautiful." He kissed her.

She still wore the strapless, ivory satin tea-length dress, with a fitted bodice covered in tiny crystals. Her bare shoulders were covered with a short matching jacket. Her new sister-in-law had taken her shopping in Denver.

She felt beautiful, too. "Yes, but I like hearing it."

He raised her hand and kissed it. "Then I'll have to say it more often."

Her husband looked incredible in his black Western-cut tuxedo. "You look mighty handsome, yourself. I saw a few women eyeing you too."

"The only woman I care about is you." He took his eyes off the highway and glanced at her. "I'm going to show you how much you mean to me tonight."

She took a shuddering breath. They'd decided to delay any honeymoon, not wanting to leave BJ. But Nola and Sylvia were going to watch BJ for this night, giving her and Jarrett time to be alone. Even though she'd gotten the all clear from Dr. Drake last week, they'd decided to wait until they were married to make love.

He went up the drive, then into the garage and pressed the button to shut out the rest of the world.

Silently, Jarrett got out of the car and walked around. Hell, he was as nervous as a teenager. He'd been wanting Mia so much the past few months, and now he wanted this night to be perfect.

He opened her door and surprised her by scooping her into his arms and carrying her into the house. He didn't stop until they were inside the dimly lit great room. He stood her in front of the French doors, but didn't let go, just leaned down and kissed her.

A kiss that soon had them breathless when he eased his mouth away.

"I love you, Mia. I can't seem to tell you enough how much I want you, tonight, and every night to come."

"I love you, too, Jarrett." She couldn't believe everything they'd gone through to get here.

How Jarrett stepped in to help her with her father. She had decided to sign over part of the company stock, but to her mother. Whatever Abigail wanted to do with it was her business. Maybe it would give her mother the courage to stand up to her husband. Even to rebuild a relationship with her daughter.

"Any regrets that I rushed you?" he asked.

"No. Have you?"

He shook his head. "Not me, but I didn't

give you much chance. I've known from the beginning you were special."

"I was attracted to you, but I blamed it on
hormones."

He cupped her face and kissed her again. "Oh,
yeah, mine are definitely working overtime. But
there's one last thing I want to give you." He
went to the desk and returned with a piece of
paper. "I've contacted my lawyer, Matt Holliston.
I introduced you to him earlier today."

"And I remember him from when we took you
to court."

Jarrett nodded. "Well, I've asked him to start
proceedings to adopt BJ."

Tears welled in her eyes. She found it hard to
speak.

"If you think it's too soon—"

She touched her finger to his lips. "I can't see
any reason not to give my son—our son a loving
father as soon as possible."

Jarrett seemed to be the one at a loss. She
loved the man who'd trusted her enough to reveal
the bad memories of his childhood. Despite all
that, or maybe because of it, he was going to
make a wonderful father for BJ.

"I love the little guy, Mia, and I love you. I
can never tell you how much."

She raised up and kissed him. "Then show
me."

There wasn't any hesitation as he swung her

up into his arms again and headed down the hall. Mia knew that with Jarrett she didn't need to run away anymore. She had him to ground her. They'd found what they needed in each other's arms.

They were home.

LARGER-PRINT BOOKS!

GET 2 FREE LARGER-PRINT NOVELS PLUS
2 FREE GIFTS!

From the Heart, For the Heart

YES! Please send me 2 FREE LARGER-PRINT Harlequin® Romance novels and my 2 FREE gifts (gifts are worth about $10). After receiving them, if I don't wish to receive any more books, I can return the shipping statement marked "cancel." If I don't cancel, I will receive 6 brand-new novels every month and be billed just $4.34 per book in the U.S. or $4.99 per book in Canada. That's a saving of 17% off the cover price! It's quite a bargain! Shipping and handling is just 50¢ per book.* I understand that accepting the 2 free books and gifts places me under no obligation to buy anything. I can always return a shipment and cancel at any time. Even if I never buy another book from Harlequin, the two free books and gifts are mine to keep forever.

186/386 HDN E7UE

Name	(PLEASE PRINT)	
Address		Apt. #
City	State/Prov.	Zip/Postal Code

Signature (if under 18, a parent or guardian must sign)

Mail to the Harlequin Reader Service:
IN U.S.A.: P.O. Box 1867, Buffalo, NY 14240-1867
IN CANADA: P.O. Box 609, Fort Erie, Ontario L2A 5X3

Not valid for current subscribers to Harlequin Romance Larger-Print books.

Are you a current subscriber to Harlequin Romance books and want to receive the larger-print edition? Call 1-800-873-8635 today!

* Terms and prices subject to change without notice. Prices do not include applicable taxes. N.Y. residents add applicable sales tax. Canadian residents will be charged applicable provincial taxes and GST. Offer not valid in Quebec. This offer is limited to one order per household. All orders subject to approval. Credit or debit balances in a customer's account(s) may be offset by any other outstanding balance owed by or to the customer. Please allow 4 to 6 weeks for delivery. Offer available while quantities last.

Your Privacy: Harlequin Books is committed to protecting your privacy. Our Privacy Policy is available online at www.ReaderService.com or upon request from the Reader Service. From time to time we make our lists of customers available to reputable third parties who may have a product or service of interest to you. If you would prefer we not share your name and address, please check here. ☐

Help us get it right—We strive for accurate, respectful and relevant communications. To clarify or modify your communication preferences, visit us at www.ReaderService.com/consumerchoice.

HRLP10R2

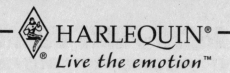